STRANGE TWIST OF FATE

Masinde Kusimba

Moran (E. A.) Publishers Limited,
Judda Complex, Prof. Wangari Maathai Road,
P. O. Box 30797, Nairobi.

With offices and representatives in: Uganda, Rwanda, Tanzania, Malawi and Zambia

www.moranpublishers.com

ISBN 978 9966 63 214 2

2016   2015   2014   2013
8   7   6   5   4   3   2   1

Prelude

Situma, twenty-five, presents himself for an interview at a city firm, Kentem Limited. He is, surprisingly, offered a job as an accountant just because Musebe, the boss, likes him on first impression. A couple of years later, the young man proves himself an ardent and industrious worker thereby winning favours and accolades from his employer. In the course of his job, he falls in love with the office secretary, Nambozo, who Musebe is also eying. The love triangle leads to his dismissal and he subsequently starts a criminal life that sees him arraigned in court and jailed. He later escapes from jail to a neighbouring country.

A new day, however, dawns for Situma when a newly elected president orders for the unconditional release of all political prisoners. His name inadvertently gets into the list of those to be pardoned. Happy to be free, Situma is met with a rude shock on his arrival home; he had long 'died' and rested in peace after word came round that he had been shot dead following a foiled robbery attempt.

A year later, after the ghosts of his presumed death are buried, Situma moves to another town where he finds himself a job as a newspaper vendor. Here, he meets and falls in love with Natasha – a rich, beautiful, young lady working for a local public relations firm.

Situma starts a new life with her and together they establish a business after quitting his newspaper vending job.

The business blossoms and the two decide to formalise their relationship. That is when he learns that Natasha is Musebe's daughter. Musebe, a former boss of Situma now turned arch-enemy, rejects his daughter's choice of a husband and swears to end their marriage plans. He maliciously schemes Situma's death but the tragedy that unfolds is more than what he had intended.

1

♦ ♦ ♦ ♦

Among those who were short-listed for the interview, the young guy felt he was the most desperate. He had visited many offices in a bid to secure any form of employment but his attempts had been futile. He had sent dozens of job applications and attended numerous interviews but did not succeed. His life, he presumed, was under control of forces; strong forces, commanding forces that were pushing him contrary to his wishes. He was staying with his uncle in the city but life was not a bed of roses either. Despite his effort, he felt like someone else was carrying out the undertaking on his behalf. The supposed *someone* did not, however, tackle his assignments completely and competently.

Situma had, therefore, opted to sit back and watch his life being dragged into an unknown destiny. The unfruitful job-seeking venture had made him lose hope in life. He turned crestfallen, disheartened and unenthusiastic about life. As he struggled, nay, as he waited in the city for his luck, his uncle's wife could not give him that peace of mind and comfort he desired most. Perhaps she enjoyed stressing him, one would say. Or simply she detested hosting job seekers, so it appeared. Her feeling was that the resources used to cater for Situma could be put to better use. As the saying goes, whoever chases you away must not necessarily say go. Situma's aunt chased him from their household in the city without telling him go. She complained bitterly whenever something, however small, went wrong and was quick to conclude that it was a result of 'living with so many people in the house.'

Here, Situma had no permission whatsoever, to do or touch anything without her consent lest he risked inviting a stream of yells and tantrums from the aunt. The unwritten law stipulated that lunch was served at 1.00 p.m. and whoever came late, even after fifteen minutes, had to wait for supper at 8.00 p.m. For a job seeker who always walked to town and came back slightly after 1.00 p.m., life was akin to sharp thorns placed on the path of a bare-footed runner.

And as Situma underwent this inhumane treatment in the hands of his aunt, his uncle did not raise a finger against it. He sat back and quietly let the woman in the house go on rampage; ruling the household with an iron fist. On several occasions, the anger that was originally aimed at Situma often spilled onto the tight-lipped uncle. Nambi never forgot to drag her husband's name into any issue, especially when she complained about Situma. She did this out of suspicion that her husband sided with Situma secretly. But much as Situma tried to please Nambi and perhaps strike a rapport with her, it all ended in vain.

One evening, Situma had just tendered his job application letter at Kentem Limited when he came back home and sat quietly in the sitting room watching the 7.00 p.m. news. His uncle had just arrived from work and was taking a shower while Nambi was in the kitchen. The kids were in the study room doing homework. Suddenly, a momentary power failure occurred lasting for barely a minute. Off then on. The television set produced a popping sound and emitted a dark-greyish smoke with an acrid smell.

Nambi came out of the kitchen with a cooking spoon in her hand and found Situma fumbling with the television set. Without asking any question, she started yelling at him, she accused the young man of having damaged it. Situma argued that the TV's electrical circuit may have been damaged due to the abrupt power surge, but this theory only served to annoy her more.

'How many times have we experienced power outages but the TV and all other electronic gadgets still work? Just shut up! Silly boy! My favourite Soap Opera is just about to begin! I have never seen such a careless, destructive hand like yours. If everyone was to behave like this then homes would not own anything. I'm fed up with this… pack your things and go back to the village tomorrow morning!' Yes, there! She at last got the opportunity to angrily spit out what she had longed to say.

In a bid to please her, Situma owned up to the accusation and apologised for the 'mistake' but this could not alter the verdict either. Quit orders had been issued and were to be obeyed. Everyone kept quiet and watched in disbelief as Situma underwent one of the most depressing moments of his life.

Nobody could speak when mama was talking and nobody could come to his defence either. Situma felt rejected with no one to run to for understanding and consolation. He wondered why God chose to let some people wallow in poverty, the so called dregs of the society, hence the top cream could ride on their backs and trample on them mercilessly. He blamed God for what he termed as 'unfair distribution of resources.'

But that evening, things had come to a head and enough was enough. Finally, the uncle who saw no evil, heard no evil and spoke no evil, eventually broke his silence.

'No, Mama Daddy you are unnecessarily taking this matter too far. Situma is my sister's son; my nephew, he looks upon us for help and guidance. It is a shame to bark at him like that and deliver such a nasty and heartless eviction notice just because of a mere TV set. He is not insane to vandalise property anyhow as you tend to imply… come on, understand this was just but a normal power hitch. In fact, tomorrow I will call the *fundi* to repair the TV, meanwhile, Situma is here to stay and will only leave at his pleasure,' the old man spoke soberly with a rare authoritative voice packed with finality.

But Nambi would not budge; a bitter exchange ensued between the two that saw children bow their heads in shame as man and wife struggled to outdo each other verbally; with each one of them lecturing the other and none of them ready to listen.

Nambi, assertively, as tears dropped from her eyes, said, 'I'm leaving this house with my kids tomorrow morning if this silly boy will not have left. And I mean it!' She then walked away into the bedroom, banged the door behind her and continued sobbing. She was always quick to shed tears during an emotional argument.

At half past midnight, when everyone in the house was sound asleep, the uncle made a rare visit to Situma's bedroom. He quietly pushed the door open without knocking. Perhaps he did not wish to disturb the kids who were asleep in the next room or possibly, he intended to make his visit a secret. Situma was in bed but had not slept yet. He was gazing idly on the ceiling board, with the evening incident weighing heavily at the back of his mind.

A visibly disturbed uncle started by apologising for interfering with the young man's sleep and then continued to encourage him not to despair in life but remain focused towards his goals. The uncle was so comforting and, with veiled terminology, he tendered his apologies to Situma over the evening uproar. He promised that such unfortunate scenes will never occur again.

However, he unveiled the message behind his midnight call. 'I want to tell you something *khocha*,' he held Situma's hand and pulled him closer as if he wanted to whisper a-million-dollar-deal to him. 'I was once a youth like you and I greatly cherished every moment of it; yes, those glorious days. Although at your age I never knew what I would become, I always remained stable and never allowed unnecessary and petty sideshows to derail me,' he said and stared at the picture of a popular European footballer (honoured as the world player of the year) pinned on Situma's wall. He was an ardent soccer fan who spent most of his time watching football matches.

After a slight pause, the uncle continued, 'Everything looked bleak but just like the sun rises at dawn and brings tremendous light upon the earth, my sun rose once and catapulted me to where I am today,' he said and smiled. Situma smiled too, nay, he simply moved his lips, without knowing precisely why and for what he was smiling at. Perhaps he had grown to dislike his uncle and the entire family.

In a typical monologue, the uncle went on, 'If anything, you have not experienced life yet; you are not employed, you are not married you have no kids, you have no dependants and virtually you have nothing to worry about in this world… you are young and fresh with a lot of potential bestowed in you. I think the one who said that life begins at forty got it right.'

But finally the message came clear, 'I don't intend to discourage your job seeking ventures but I wish to suggest that you take a short break, go home and relax a bit then come back and see what the world has in store for you. Just go home… visit mum and dad, then come back after a month or so to pursue your employment opportunities, this time with renewed vigour,' he said and pressed a Sh1,000 note in the young man's palm. Yes, the uncle had yielded to Nambi's demands and threats. Situma had to leave.

The following morning Situma woke up early at the time children were preparing for school and started packing his belongings. He had nothing much to pack anyway, and within 10 minutes, he was done. A small bag with a handful of clothes was all he had. When his uncle's children noticed that their closest pal who always spared a shilling to buy them sweets and play with them during the weekends, teaching and entertaining them was leaving, they jammed his room and expressed their outrage at his sudden departure. 'Don't go, stay with us,' they cried.

At least the eldest boy, commonly known as Daddy because he was named after his father's father, precisely knew their mother had chased Situma away. After all, he clearly heard and understood everything that transpired in the sitting room the previous evening.

The little girl, who fondly referred to Situma as Big Brother, because he was the biggest brother around anyway, cried uncontrollably, seeking to accompany him. It took the house help a hell of time to convince the little girl that Situma was only going to town and would be back in the evening. 'But why is he carrying his bag?' she was quick to ask.

When he reached the bus park, Situma was about to board a bus to Kinambi but thought twice about it. Should I go home? What will I do at home? He sat on a bench and debated whether or not to travel to the village. Finally, he chose to remain in the city.

Back at home he was not accorded the status that befitted a young man of his calibre. He did not even own a small cubical, *simba*, that formed the pride of his peers. His father's farm was not sufficient to enable him practice agriculture either. The two acres of land his family was settled on by the State under the famous *Masikini* Settlement Schemes in Namufweli village, Kinambi County, could not in any way help him generate income that could spur economic development. Situma, therefore, resolved not to go home, to a home of nothing. He was at least better off in the city because he had a distant and vague hope of securing casual employment in one of the industrial firms.

One of his close friends, Watima, was working as an Accountant at Miami Financial Scheme. Situma visited him in the office that morning and gave him a detailed explanation of the drama at the uncle's place. 'I have been kicked out,' he lamented. Watima was sympathetic and he offered to stay with him in his single room as he went about looking for employment.

'It is tricky to survive in the city with a relative,' said Watima.

*   *   *

Finally, one day, the good news arrived; Situma had been short-listed for an interview at Kentem Limited in Karoko. Thus, that morning as he waited at the reception, his heart kept throbbing fast as he wondered what the outcome of this interview would be. He expected the worst but hoped for the best. After all, he had attended many interviews and got so many disappointments that this would just be one of the many heart-breaks. Besides getting used to disappointments, he believed one lost nothing in trying.

He was the first to be called into the Manager's office. He knocked lightly on the door and entered; facing a bald-headed and well build man seated alone in a spacious office, swinging in a chair as he spoke on the phone. There was no interview panel here, Situma noticed. Musebe looked at his certificates and asked a handful of questions about the young man's background: where he grew up, academic history, professional and work background and what he was presently engaged in.

Situma conducted himself well during the interview, answering all the questions to the manager's satisfaction. Without much ado and formalities the boss posed, 'Do you think you are the person this company is looking for?'

'Yes, I believe I'm capable of dealing with the challenges posed by the job,' Situma responded.

'Then take it and work hard. I'm advised against judging a book by its cover but today, I have taken the risk of doing that. Simply, I mean, by observing your character, I'm convinced that you can make a reliable and trusted employee.'

Situma could not believe his ears. Everything had worked out right for him, beyond expectations. At last he had secured a job. 'What a good and affable boss, what a godsend, considerate and fatherly man,' Situma thought. He, nonetheless, felt like he was dreaming; perhaps he would wake up and find himself jobless again as everything proved a bitter joke!

Everyone in the world seemed against him but only Musebe appeared to be on his side.

'I have entrusted my confidence in you and it will be your duty to work and prove your worth in our organisation. Will you do that?' the boss inquired casually while moving round in his comfortable chair.

'I'm sure we are going to get along well. I'll give this company all my best,' he assured the boss. He could, however, hear voices in his head murmuring 'tread carefully Situma' so he decided to be cautious.

'Is the interview over?' he wondered while fighting not to give way to the wild excitement that cropped up in him, which made him feel like jumping up and dancing. The heaven-sent luck made him suddenly acquire some air of self importance. He viewed himself as superior and more blessed than all other job-seekers in the world. He had walked into the interview while unsettled but he now sat relaxed and could feel a sigh of relief, for once.

The rest of the interviewees were called in one by one and given an oral interview as a formality, though the vacancy they were craving for had already been awarded to Situma.

'Come in... what is your name... OK, your original particulars... I see... where do you come from?' These were some of the questions posed by Musebe who in the end told them to leave their contacts so that they could be contacted later in case one of them was picked for the position.

All said and done, it was Situma's star that shone brightest at the end of the day. The appointment took place with immediate effect and he was asked to report on duty the following morning. The positive turn of events made him deliriously happy.

2

◆ ◆ ◆ ◆

For the first two years of his employment, everything went on smoothly and Situma did his job with lots of contentment, vigour and enthusiasm. He was an excellent and reliable accountant and the boss liked him so much. Consequently, in one of the management meetings, Musebe suggested a salary increment for effective workers, with specific reference to Situma. Musebe termed him the best performer and whenever an exemplary comment came from the boss, Situma's name was always mentioned.

His loyalty to the boss further led to him being trusted with large sums of money, especially when it came to banking, withdrawals and managing the company's funds. Their closeness and what could be seen as teamwork was exhibited when the boss often took him out for lunch and occasionally bought him a drink after work.

With his roving eye, however, Musebe did not give a chance to ladies who came his way. He was quick to woo them into a relationship. Since Kentem Limited hired Nambozo as a receptionist, Musebe eyed her lustfully. And just like an eagle waits patiently to pounce on its prey, the boss waited apprehensively for an opportune time to unleash his wiles on her.

Nambozo was a light, slim lady of medium height. She appeared shy in character and always monitored every step she made. She was twenty-five years old. She spoke fluent English and never uttered words carelessly. Though she was chatty, her words were always calculated and came with a solid purpose – save for some little hearty jokes here and there with friends. She usually won the hearts of many potential admirers. She was the type Situma once described as 'a gem that God created cautiously, slowly, step by step without any hurry whatsoever.'

One day Musebe summoned her in his office and remarked passionately, 'Nambozo your office work is good, I'm impressed. I like your filing system… Since you came here order has manifested itself in this office.'

'Thank you very much Sir, that is my duty,' she replied gleefully.

'I guess what we see here in the office reflects the kind of person you are back at home. I have a feeling that your house and the items therein are organised in a manner that encourages visitors not to want to leave,' he said and burst into a lengthy bossy laughter… 'One of these days I should visit you.'

Nambozo smiled too but was not amused. The boss further posed a rather friendly question, 'Tell me something about yourself, how do you spend your leisure time? I guess you enjoy going out, partying with friends and meeting nice folks out there for a drink and general social networking?'

'Yes, I enjoy going out with friends once in a while, say once a month,' she answered but became suspicious as to why the boss was getting concerned about her private life.

'I hope you don't mind accompanying me this evening to a get-together party at Karoko Members Club? I have been invited to a corporate dinner and I would wish you accompany me. It will give you an opportunity to rub shoulders with the top cream of the society... Trade and Industry Cabinet Secretary is among the invited dignitaries...'

'Thank you for the offer Mr. Musebe... but I won't be able to come... I have to stand in for my aunt and do some house chores this evening... she is not feeling well.'

'Look here Nambozo you are a grown up. You need to do your things with total independence. Someone should not hold you captive at home and hinder your private programmes... doesn't she have a house help? Call and tell her that you will not turn up at home as expected.'

'No please, Mr. Musebe, I owe her a lot. She is my guardian and I will always do everything to make her happy. I am what I am because of her.'

'But I can make you become what you had never imagined you would become. Yes, I'm capable of transforming you overnight to the status of a princess. This humble outing will create for you a lifetime opportunity to make great fortunes and be able to stand on your own as a mature and independent woman... and you will owe allegiance to yourself, you see... yourself, not anybody. Come on, think about it.'

Nambozo came short of sneering at him and walking out of his office but she composed herself. She was annoyed, very annoyed. She wondered why the respectable boss had chosen to tell her all that, anyway.

Musebe stood from his chair and came round the table where she was. She got frightened. 'You are such a pretty woman and I believe you know these things better than I do. I don't want it to look like I'm forcing you into this affair. With all your wonderful physical endowment; in fact you're the most beautiful and irresistible lady I've ever come across lately, you should not be the type that struggles to make ends meet,' he said and looked at Nambozo but she was still not amused.

He continued making his wild promises, 'I will provide for you anything you want, anything, when you want it, where you want it; just mention it and you'll get it. Young men are out there seeking your love and they will speak all kinds of *dry* words to make you fall victim of their malicious traps. Many girls have been in this sorry state before but I would like to save your name from being added to this regrettable list… I really love you Nambozo.'

'No. It's not possible. You are a family man and I don't want to wreck families. Besides, I respect you as my father owing to your age… I mean, you are better suited to be my father and not my lover.'

'Be sober in your words, this affair is strictly between you and me and not you and my family or any other party. My age is just but a number. I'm still young at heart, you know. But that aside, whatever I will offer you is what matters,' he lowered his voice and whispered, 'I will buy you a house in one of the posh estates in the city, where you will live exclusively… I will make sure you are the most comfortable woman.' Nambozo did not say anything. She just stood unmoved. Bored. Scared. Annoyed. Frustrated.

'Anyway this is a long lasting matter, take your time and we will discuss it later but I urge you to look at it positively.'

Nambozo left Musebe's office regretting the day she joined the organisation. The boss was using his position and wealth to lure her into an affair that she deemed futureless. Moreover, it was her resolve not to fall in love or even hang out with married or elderly men who were of her father's age. Had Musebe seen an easy catch that could be trapped by the dangle of a shilling?

Over the weekend, she visited her friend and former college mate, Robina, to borrow some music CDs. As usual with ladies, they engaged in girlish talk, gossiping about men. Robina spoke at length about her boyfriend and how their relationship was doomed to fail due to what she termed as his 'continued infidelity.' She blamed him so much for wrecking their three-year-old relationship by flirting with other ladies and bluntly confessed she was now searching for a better suitor.

Since Musebe made advances at her, Nambozo had never shared the experience with anyone. She needed someone understanding to share her confusion with and perhaps get some guidance. Her aunt was not the best person to speak to on such matters, she preferred an agemate.

Thus, she decided to tell Robina what transpired in the office.

'Robina, let me tell you something ridiculous. My boss is shamelessly asking for my hand in love! He is too old and besides that I absolutely have no feelings for him. I turned him down recently but he insisted so much and advised me to think about the matter positively. If he keeps insisting again, I will have no choice but to quit the company… I'll just walk away,' Nambozo lamented.

Robina looked at her, surprised, and then broke into a long feminine laughter with a tinge of ridicule.

'I never knew you are that naive. Open your eyes to opportunities. You are pretty and that means high-class personalities will always knock on your door imploring you to open and let them settle in your heart. I don't expect you to be foolish to reject such a generous and lifetime proposal from a guy who has money and is willing to spend it on you. Come on, little girl, rush to the office on Monday morning and tell the big man that you are sorry for what happened!'

Nambozo looked at her and sneered. She wondered if Robina had gone insane. 'Are you suggesting that I can as well be a sugar daddy's concubine? Style up please,' she sneered, stood up and threatened to walk away. One thing was certain, she was disappointed in Robina.

'Hey come on, this world is a competitive one, it's the kind of place where everyone struggles for the best. Even Julio Iglesias, Spanish singer spelt it out candidly in his hit song *Love is on Our Side Again* that 'In this crazy life, let us reach for the best we can.' We all wish to eat the best meals, get the best salaries, hook up with best guys, stay in the best houses, dress exclusively and drive the best cars… just the best of everything. This translates into one thing – money. Get a guy who has money and stick to him for that's all it takes. A ride on your boss' humble back will guarantee job security, promotion and all other advantages that come with such connections,' said Robina.

'Stop! *Bona kuno,* your sentiments are mean. It's utterly wrong to look at one's financial muscle as the basis for a relationship. Consider the age factor too. This guy is old enough to be my dad. He has children who are our agemates… and I don't love him. My parents, my brothers and my sisters expect a lot from me. They expect to see me married soon… and none of them will be comfortable with the choice of an old hubby. And being a second or a third wife is the most daunting ridicule. I need to pick someone I can be proud of, someone I can introduce to my family members without fear or hesitation. I don't want to be a disgrace to my parents either,' retorted Nambozo.

'Definitely you need someone to keep you company. You need a man; a man of means to settle down with not just any ordinary man. By the way, how strong is your relationship with the other chap you once said you work with? I don't even remember his name.'

'He is called Situma. I'm not in a relationship with him yet. We have not discussed anything about love but he is such a nice guy to be with and in case he makes a proposal, I will consider him,' Nambozo assured her.

'Does he have what it takes? Is he a man of means? Is he rich? Does he drive or is he simply the type that walks to the office every morning carrying with him the entire street dust and sweat? I just don't have a taste for such lousy fellows… Nowadays it is a matter of *nipe nikupe.*'

'I never knew you are such a trivial thinking woman. Your preferences are blind and the sooner you review them the better. You cannot love someone because of money! That is ridiculous, miserably artificial and pretentious. What happens when he runs broke?' posed Nambozo.

But Robina had a different opinion altogether: 'Nambozo, you must understand there is no romance without finance. You need money to nurture and develop love. You need money to go places while courting, to buy presents that manifest love and generally patron a five-star hotel and feel the sweetness of love and life. Gone are the days when men spoke *empty* words and terribly won many fair hearts. In this era, the highest bidder carries the day,' Robina said and implored her friend to stop living in the past and face the reality called 'modernity.'

'Money is vital in a relationship, but it should not come primarily. Love should be the overriding factor and then finance can come in second, but not the reverse. Money can only be an overriding factor if one is a sex worker, but that is not what is in my mind, I don't intend to sell myself…'

'But one thing my friend, remember the past is gone, forget about it; the future is yet to come, don't worry about it; the present is here, utilise it.' This was Robina's parting shot. From the chat, it was clear none of them was willing to give in. Each one seemed to hold tight on their convictions and principles. The more they argued, the more they disagreed. Nambozo went back to her house more confused than she came. It had been quite some time since she met and talked to Robina, and now she kept wondering how spoilt, reckless and immoral her friend had become.

3

◆ ◆ ◆ ◆

Walking through the valley of the shadow of death, he literally felt a liquid drop into his stomach. A human corpse, with its mouth wide open, was lying on his path. Surrounding the body were scattered skulls and skeletons of human beings. Situma felt like he had been thrown into a bottomless abyss. He tried to find out where he was but the eerie surrounding was stomach wrenching; he was in the middle of nowhere.

He racked his brains about the issue but his thoughts literally backfired. Many questions came to his mind but went unanswered. He turned round and saw a huge figure of an indefinite size, a monster. Its face resembled that of a human being but it had numerous large horns on its head and protruding teeth like those of a warthog. His nerves froze. He tried to run but all in vain; his legs were too heavy. He tried to shout for help but no sound came out.

The ghoulish ogre started advancing towards him; closer and closer in sinister, deliberate and authoritative manner, just like an eagle approaches a lonely chick in a bare field. Situma was not bold enough to face the murderous ogre. He had to scamper in fear to escape the ordeal and thank God he managed to run to safety, so he thought.

He ran frantically not knowing where he was bound, for he took the opposite direction hoping that he was evading the horrific monster only to find that he was heading towards it! In an eye-twinkling flash, he changed the course making a complete turn, but again, he saw the ogre waiting for him in the direction he was dashing to. Hoping against hope, he tried to escape but poor him, there was no way out.

The ghostly creature proved omnipresent, so Situma yielded to it and became like an insect trapped in the stigma of an insectivorous plant. He collapsed due to great shock and lay unconscious waiting for his death which looked very certain. 'Lord, take me back safely as I come home,' he absent-mindedly managed to mutter a prayer.

The ogre now had its clumsy, magical hands and teeth wide open ready to make a feast out of him; an easy prey. As it stretched its muscular hands to grab him and consequently devour him, Situma disengaged himself and, thank God, he miraculously woke up, sweating all over.

With a hagridden face, he sat on his bed, sighed heavily and shook his head in total disbelief. The terrible dream made him look awry, sickly and very weary. For once he appeared very aged. Thoughtfully, he reviewed the miserable dream and attempted to establish its horoscopic connotations. His eyes darted from one corner of the wall to another, traversing across the roof, flying over the wall pictures, searching for an elusive answer. Eventually they landed on the wall clock: it was 8:15 am. He was late for work.

He prepared hurriedly and set off at a lightning speed. He caught the most convenient bus that manoeuvred through the morning traffic jam – breaking all the traffic rules

– and within fifteen minutes, he was already at the city centre; about 100 metres from Nameme Plaza where their offices were situated. In the office, Situma met Nambozo perusing through a file that contained some important company documents. She greeted him with a smile and he also answered back with a broad grin.

Outside, the weather was piercingly chilly. The dark nimbus clouds made the atmosphere look gloomy. Nine o'clock in the morning appeared like 6.00 a.m. Clouds had covered the morning sun and a thin line of disappearing mist could be seen everywhere. Situma had gone to the office wishing that Musebe was away.

'Is the *Proprietor* around?' he asked Nambozo in a whisper. That is the name that workers called their boss here.

'Yah, he's in... I got this file for him.'

'Has he asked for me?'

'Nope.'

'And what are you searching for? I can see you are so serious,' Situma remarked in a husky voice.

'Well, he wants me to get him some agreement deeds over the renting out of our business premises in Usoko town,' she answered and quipped, 'You must have woken up on the wrong side this morning. You look so bored, rather worried... or is it a hangover? Situma, what's not happening?' she asked rather concerned with a seductive smile.

Her concern, or whatever it was, cheered his troubled mind. He became happy and quite jumpy. Despite this, he felt it needless to narrate to her the horrible morning dream, instead, he smiled vaguely and said, 'There is nothing wrong, don't mistake my looks for boredom or hangover either, that is my usual facial appearance – it's the way God created me.' Nambozo could not hold back a laughter; she unleashed it loudly.

Situma was still sharing with her the morning glory when the boss emerged from his office and found them in high spirits. Was it Nambozo's laughter that fished him out? Did he intend to know why she was laughing and with whom… or was he perhaps on his way out?

That morning Musebe wore a gloomy face that made him appear more of a ghost than a human being. This reminded Situma of the ghosts that terrorised him in the dream. The boss was so grumpy and extremely annoyed as evidenced by his wrinkled face. Even the fury that Pharaoh, the ancient king of Egypt, had after the sons of Israel were driven out of his Kingdom could not match Musebe's. The anger made his tie appear like a hangman's noose around his neck.

'Good morning, Sir,' Situma greeted him though he knew the boss was not in the mood of exchanging pleasantries. And true, Musebe ignored Situma and addressed Nambozo straight away thundering, 'Have you found those documents?'

'Not yet, Sir,' she said flipping through the file, leaf after leaf.

'Alas! What the hell is this? You ought to have found them by now precisely. I require them urgently before the board meeting begins. I gave out this assignment long time ago - almost half an hour – but you are just here laughing for no good reason,' Musebe coughed out angrily.

'And you,' the boss turned to Situma, 'today we have a board meeting. Make sure you hand in your monthly report this morning. I expect a detailed report, no short cuts especially for a busy month like the just ended one.'

Situma sighed heavily. The boss could notice the surprise on his face; he had not prepared it. Indeed he was not aware that the monthly report was needed so urgently and early like this. Worse still, he was not aware of the meeting of executives scheduled for this morning.

Situma had carried all the relevant documents to his house the day before with the intention of drafting the crucial report but his meeting with Watima at a local pub did not give room for work. He got drunk and forgot about it only to be reminded by the boss now.

Often, as they say, when disaster looms at your doorsteps it is easier to sense it but you may not comprehend it, for it brings a dark spell to encase your mind and confuse you further before dealing you the final death blow. And as physicians say, it happens in hectic fever; that at the beginning of a malady, it is easy to cure but difficult to detect, but in the course of time, not having been detected or treated in the beginning, it becomes easy to detect but difficult to cure. Situma had carried some documents to his apartment with the intention of preparing a monthly report because he had sensed some danger, the malady was beginning, but he took the matter lightly. Now he is in trouble. Will he survive the ordeal as the fire burns underneath?

'Are you through with the report?' Musebe asked for confirmation. Truth sometimes kills, so Situma decided to tell his boss a lie.

'I completed it days ago. Accidentally, I carried it away home among other personal documents and I forgot it there,' said Situma.

'I don't expect you to be such nonsensical. Do you have another office somewhere else?'

'No, Sir, the document is in my house. I was in a hurry this morning so I… ' Situma tried to give a panicky excuse but he was cut short.

'So you have moved to a new office in your house? Has your square room turned into a Kentem office? Hurry up and bring the report now! Next time I will not tolerate the inconveniences you are causing us!' Musebe's loud, angry voice literally sent the door creaking and the walls shaking.

The secretary's computer also appeared to be dancing. Situma, could not help fearing that an earthquake had struck the place. He remembered some folktales that were narrated to him long time ago, during his childhood days, about a kingdom chief who, when he heard that his soldiers had been defeated in a battle with the neighbouring clan, and a bigger percentage of them killed, he summoned the commander and reprimanded him so angrily, loudly and bitterly until the strongly built roof of the palace collapsed and fell on him (the chief) and the subjects; killing them instantly. Situma related this king to Musebe. Will the walls of this office collapse and kill us too? He stormed out of the office in a huff and rushed to pick a *matatu* to Marai. He hurried up purposely to go and prepare the report hastily, say for one hour, and later on lie to the boss that their vehicle broke down causing the delay.

The *matatu* cruised at a rather breakneck speed but to Situma, it was crawling and he thought of getting out and running to the house. At last they reached Marai. He dipped into his jacket pocket to retrieve his keys but realised they were missing. He had forgotten them on Nambozo's desk in the office. He got flabbergasted; his heart skipped a beat, he almost fainted.

He breathed hard and kicked the door in annoyance and sheer frustration. He leaned on the door helplessly and groaned inwardly because since the day began, everything he did seemed to end up in a cul-de-sac. He prayed to God asking Him to miraculously open the door for him, the way he stopped the flow of the Red Sea and allowed the children of Israel to cross, but no miracle happened. Such were the moments – rare moments and hard moments – when Situma sought God's intervention.

Steady but surely, the clock was ticking. Standing and staring could not provide a solution either. With little time remaining to hand in the report, he was either to go back to the office for his keys or break the door. He opted for the latter and then hire a carpenter to repair it later. After borrowing a hammer from Kamari, a carpenter in his neighborhood, Situma set on dismantling his door lock. It was made of steel and he had to master all his energy to shatter it. The loud bang attracted the attention of the patrol policemen who were passing by.

'That must be a thief!' exclaimed one of the cops. They slowed down their vehicle and peered at him. Situma continued hitting the lock harder than before without showing any signs of guilt. He turned his head and saw a policeman walking towards him. What's up with this damn bugger? Situma wondered. The idea of escaping did not occur to him for he knew he was at the right place, at the right time, doing the right thing.

Unbelievably, the cop grabbed him by the collar with the agility of a mountain goat and gave him a blinding slap across the face before frog-matching him into a waiting *black-maria*. The hammer fell a considerable distance away but the policeman did not care to pick it up as evidence for prosecution; if ever they were to prosecute him, anyway.

Within no time Situma had been squeezed into a dark cabin and could not raise a voice to defend himself. He could not even recall how he got there; but he was there. Around him were several shaggy, rugged men with scary faces and imposing physiques. *'Must be murderers, yes, organised terrorist groups,'* he thought. Besides him were police officers clutching their G-3 guns, others with AK-47, with their fingers tapping menacingly on the trigger. Do they want to shoot us? This sight and thought made Situma tremble.

Situma considered himself as a harmless man not suitable to be in such a place guarded by heavily armed officers. He tried to explain the truth of the matter to a policeman who appeared senior in rank hoping he would release him unconditionally, but that was not to be.

'The house is mine…but my key got…'

'Weeh kijana…' he was cut short, 'Look at this daylight robber, daring and confident. Just keep quiet. How many incidents of this nature we handled? Nowadays robbers like you are very confident, you break into locked houses claiming you are the rightful owners when actual owners are

out at work. We shall keep you behind bars until you are proven not guilty. You cannot confuse us over this.' Situma tried again to talk to a different police officer but all his efforts to have them listen were futile.

'I'm sorry you are saying the right thing to the wrong person at the wrong time. Spare your words and breath so that when time is ripe you will speak to the judge in court. Our work is to arrest, give *discipline* and arraign you in a court of law. We do not listen to fabrications and crippled excuses of your kind,' the officer asserted and smiled furtively. It was more of a slight movement of the lips than a smile. This irritated Situma more.

But what could he do? He clearly saw the futility of arguing with the officers, the most rigid and incorrigible fellows, as he termed them. So he tried to be as humble as possible to prove his innocence which he was apparently sure would work for him. He never attempted to gaze into their eyes amid the assertions that he was a robber because that could have aggravated the situation. After all, it's usually the very brave or the very stupid and those completely ignorant of routine prison torture that dare gaze straight into the police officer's eyes either to challenge them or to question their authority. Situma belonged to neither of the calibres, so he kept mum and waited for his fate.

'*How could I break into my own house to rob myself? Why do these damned nincompoops hate the voice of reason? Can't they listen to what I'm telling them… or do they think I can't own such a good house?*' He wondered. He thought of Musebe and the monthly report saga. '*This may mark the end of my contract with Kentem Limited.*'

He sank deep into thoughts; the home people and the much they depended on him for school fees and general upkeep. His rent, food and other basic requirements were bound to hang in the balance. But when the going gets tough the tough gets going, so he consoled himself. 'Even if Musebe sacks me I don't care… I believe I can still survive, I'm a hardcore…'

Suddenly, a piercing cane landed across his back, startling him.

'What are you talking about?' the cynical police officer who flogged him asked. In defiance, Situma did not speak a word.

'You are claiming to be a hardcore, you think we can't break that hardcore of yours? We've often broken the hardest cores ever seen.' They had misunderstood Situma.

'Let us reach the station first, I will beat the rudeness out of your head and you will sing – if speaking is hard,' the cop threatened him.

The police were notorious for torturing suspects and a good number of people had died mysteriously while in police custody due to beating, so Situma was careful lest he could fall victim of their brutality. He remembered the case of Mukhebo, a fiery political activist who was arrested by the police for allegedly speaking ill of the ruling regime. And as he waited to be arraigned in court for tramped up charges related to treason, he was taken out in the company of other suspects to cut grass in the police station's compound.

The four slashers available were not enough for the five suspects and it was Mukhebo who missed the cutting tool.

The cops forced him to use his hands or teeth to cut the grass! With his political defiance, Mukhebo declined to take the orders, citing political harassment and told the police that he knew his rights as a suspect and further argued he was not supposed to take any kind of punishment until proven guilty and sentenced by the court.

'Hey, man, you're trying to be smart… eeh … today you'll realise that one is guilty until proven innocent,' a policeman said and forced him down on his knees, ordering him to chew grass! But Mukhebo was unable to undertake the exercise effectively like a herbivore. The cop, swearing to teach him a lesson, hit him hard on the back with the rifle butt, fatally injuring his spinal cord. The political activist collapsed but nobody bothered to attend to him. The police officers within the compound looked at the incident and laughed.

After about three hours without medical attention, Mukhebo's state worsened. The police reluctantly took him to the hospital but he died on the way and his body was dumped in a public morgue.

A committee which comprised of policemen was formed to conduct inquiries into the politician's death. Their report, released six months later, summarily stated that Mukhebo was trying to escape from police custody and injured his spinal cord fatally when he jumped over the fence and landed into a ditch. The fear and hatred for police was borne out of such degree of brutality and misuse of power. The force's motto humbly stated *Service for All*, but their general deeds contradicted this blueprint. The law enforcers became notorious law breakers. The cops had the mandate of keeping law and order but unfortunately they championed acts of lawlessness to an extent that they collaborated with thugs or were sometimes thugs themselves.

It was said in Karoko City and other towns across the country that at least four out of ten thugs that terrorised residents were police officers, and that guns used by criminals were often hired from the police. Instead of maintaining peace and order in society, the police went round causing chaos, harassing innocent people and using firearm in unwarranted manner. It was common to hear that someone had been shot for consuming illicit brew, *enguli*.

The *blackmaria* arrived at the police station and all the netted suspects of different kinds were ordered out – with tight shackles round their arms – and booked into a remand cell. Situma was in the company of other criminals who had been picked on the way, among them a mob justice victim who was saved by the appearance of the cops. His case was a true Scylla and Charybdis: jumping from the wrath of mob justice into police torture. He had snatched a purse from a woman in the market but did not make away with it; he was captured. Hardly had the crowd set on him with kicks, blows and stones than the police officers reached the scene. They fired in the air and managed to rescue him from an irate mob baying for his blood. Now he was headed for more trouble in the gaol.

In the police cells at Marai, Situma's heart throbbed fast. Inmates termed Situma as a weak gangster; a mouse that attempted to wrestle with a cat; a mosquito that dared an elephant for a public contest; and so on. In spite of all this jeers and name-callings, Situma humbly absorbed all the stinging remarks without a repartee. In a solemn mood he contemplated Psalms 23: *Even if I walk through the valley of the shadow of death, I will not be afraid...*

Some inmates appeared to sympathise with him but the way they expressed their sympathy was not genuine; they mocked him rather. Wangwe, one of the sympathisers of Situma, said: 'Sorry my man for having been locked up here despite your innocence, but remember this cage is meant for human beings, not wild animals and I'm certainly pleased that you are one of them; an image of God, in fact, divinity tells us so.'

A teenage boy who seemed to enjoy life in prison told Situma, 'You are my friend, when they bring food you will add me your share. They're about to bring lunch now, I like today's food... maize and beans...'

But Situma could not imagine himself in a police cell rubbing shoulders with hardened criminals to whom this was a way of life. He remembered the incident of Paul and Silas in the Bible and prayed to God that the same may happen to him. 'If this door opens and the guards sleep, I will shoot out and run as fast as my legs will allow me. I won't talk to anybody.'

At about 2.30 p.m., a policeman came into the cells and called out his name, 'Situma Wanami!' It was as loud as a trumpet of the angel of doom announcing the end of the world.

'Yes,' he responded.

'You fool, they say *Afande*,' an inmate corrected him.

That's none of my business, Situma was about to shout back but changed his mind against engaging in a verbal contest with miserable souls that had been condemned to rot in jail.

'Mr. Wanami,' the cop addressed him honourably after taking him out of the remand cell. 'Your crime is a very serious one, and if you appear in court, even with the shrewdest lawyer in town for your defence, you will still be sentenced to jail for not less than five years…,' he said and stared directly into Situma's eyes, perhaps to allow the gravity of the doomsday message to sink deeper. Situma shied away, bored and annoyed. The policeman was carrying a penal code in his hand. He opened it and read a section that went: 'Any person who attempts to break into a building with intent to steal is liable to…' Situma looked at the cop inattentively. 'This damn bastard is reading to me the punishment of a crime I know nothing about.'

After reading the clause and the sentence due, the cop whispered, 'I don't want you to undergo all this pain and even lose your job as well, so *jitetee bwana.*' He demanded a Sh. 500 bribe. Situma fished out a Sh. 1000 note from his breast pocket, lying between yesterday's lunch receipts and handed it over to him, perhaps hoping to get back his change. Another cop, however, intervened and announced rudely, '*Kijana, hakuna* change!'

'And where did you steal the money?' he went on asking.

'I didn't steal, I worked for it!' Situma answered with a slight temper building up in him though he feared to exchange words with them lest he got locked in afresh for other new charges. He knew that he lived in a society where people clapped for those who slapped them, where people praised those who stole from them and where people cheered those that trampled on their rights. Man eateth man, the society was.

'You can go now, you are free but don't break into people's houses again. The law will deal with you ruthlessly.' As he walked out of the police station, Situma harboured a host of mixed feelings. He was happy and relieved for gaining back his freedom. At the same time, he nursed frustrations and bitterness for having been unjustifiably inconvenienced by the police and robbed of his cash for no apparent reason. Worse still, he was scared of Musebe's reaction to his disappearance. Will the boss read insubordination or absconding duty?

CHAPTER
4

◆ ◆ ◆ ◆

Time check, 4.00 p.m. Situma had just been released from police custody twenty-five kilometres away from the city and was making his way to the office. He wanted to meet Musebe and spell out his day's predicament; to explain why he could not hand in his monthly report on time. He also wanted to pick his house keys from the office. On alighting from a *matatu,* he met Nambozo in the street on her way home.

'You went forever, what happened?'

'Any news? May be *Mr. Proprietor* has...'

'Nothing new,' he just remained silent and gloomy the whole morning and did not come back after lunch. Their meeting was called off immediately you left. One of the directors had a pressing personal matter and another one also sent his apologies too,' Nambozo informed him.

'The going has been very tough for me today. Since morning I've been to hell and back; traversing trails of hot coal, temptations and suffering. I will live to curse this day,' Situma said. Again, as if startled from a nap, he asked, 'Where are my keys?'

'They're here,' she said and retrieved them from her handbag, 'I was bringing them over to your place,' added

Nambozo though she did not even know where Situma resided.

Situma quickly understood the statement to mean that he was at least in her mind. He told her about his day's misery which he termed 'the police encounter.' Though not a superstitious man, he vaguely related the day's events to the mysterious dream he had the night before.

'Oh dear, these are mere temptations of the world as you said; the world is revealing its true colours. But you must strive to overcome trials because they are inevitable. After all, it is written in the holy book that happy are the sufferers for they shall bounce back to glory,' Nambozo consoled him. Situma could not remember the last time he heard such motivational sentiments.

'Please, Nambozo, join me for a cup of coffee if you don't mind,' he offered her an evening treat.

'Well, but make sure you don't delay me there. I have some other commitments this evening.'

'Of course we shall be there briefly, I promise,' he assured her as they walked to one of their favourite joints in the city.

In the café, they sat in a secluded corner and placed their order, coffee. The excitement in him and the presence of Nambozo by his side made him forget all the problems he had faced, the ones surrounding him and those due to come. He leaned on her, held his hand across her shoulder possessively and whispered, 'Nambozo, I love you.'

'Eer, Situma stop cheating me,' she responded shyly.

'No, my dear, I really mean what I say... and I say what I mean. You're my dream woman. All my hopes are banked on you. Without you being beside me, my life would be very unexciting…'

'*Wacha*, men are liars. They talk good but mean evil. And, sadly, they always tell the same thing to dozens of women,' Nambozo challenged him.

The two talked at length about their family backgrounds and personal experiences during college days and past love-life. They also discussed the importance of being faithful in a romantic relationship and the advantages of being in love with a serious partner. They left the café at 8.00 p.m. and took a cab to Situma's house in Marai. That evening, Situma found it weird to accept that he had been detained in police cells for some hours and only set free after offering a bribe.

'This amuses me, what if I had no money?' he wondered.

'I would have been charged for breaking into my own house to rob myself. I could have been a plaintiff as well as the defendant! The judge would read, Situma Wanami you are hereby accused of conspiring with malice aforethought to break into the house of one Situma Wanami intending to steal…' They both burst into laughter as he fumbled with the legal jargon.

By and large, the cell incident weighed heavily on his mind. Still he could not believe he had offered a bribe to cover up something he did not do. 'If papa gets to know this he can disown me as his son,' he got worried.

Situma's father, *Mzee* Wanami, a pastor at Namufweli Friends Church, was widely known as a man who strongly detested and stood against corrupt ways. This was practically witnessed when Situma completed his

Diploma in Accountancy course. A supposedly well-connected individual wanted to secure him a job in one of the famous shipping companies at the Coast on condition that they bribe their way through.

When Wanami heard of the deal, he warned his son to let go the whole issue. Much as he had no money to bribe, he hated corruption in its entirety. Perhaps this stand was as a result of many years of acquaintance with the church missionaries who discouraged among other vices, corruption. The *Mzee* had tried as much as possible to bring up his children in a morally sound way despite the general state of poverty that hit him hard. Despite everything else, he still could not allow things to get out of hand; he always stepped in to advise and patronise his son. This pastor never lost hope in life, however tough the conditions were. He always fought and struggled with hard situations to the end, his words being; 'be strong in faith like David, God is with you, and down will Goliath go.'

A bad beginning makes a good ending and after every calamity, comes relief. That evening, Situma did not go to the bar. He stayed in the house after the trying encounter and compiled the monthly report (which was the cause of all misery) as Nambozo prepared supper.

*   *   *

The following morning Musebe sent for Situma. 'The boss wants to meet you,' Nambozo relayed the message to him through the inter-com. He stood up, adjusted his tie and crossed over to the boss' office carrying the monthly report with him.

'Will the boss give me a nice treatment as he did when I came looking for employment two years ago? I think he won't be harsh if I present him this report and exaggerate the problems I faced yesterday. I hope he understands.' He muttered a prayer: 'Lord be with me and tell the boss that I didn't intend it, amen.'

Situma tapped slightly on Musebe's door, turned the handle and entered. He stood facing the boss perhaps waiting to be ushered to a seat.

'Mr. Wanami, you have become such a mischievous fellow! Do you know why you were recruited in this organisation?' asked a visibly angry Musebe. Frightened, Situma did not say a word. He forced an apologetic smile but this appeared to annoy the boss more.

'You're laughing! Yesterday you wasted the whole day, a full working day! Is this your private enterprise where you pop in and exit as you wish?' Musebe spat out angrily and gazed directly into Situma's eyes. Since he discovered that Situma was seeking Nambozo's hand in love, and that Nambozo was likely to respond positively, Musebe began to hate him passionately for creating competition. He had been looking for an opportunity to pour scorn on the young man.

An uncomfortable silence followed. Situma tried to defend himself but he was cut short immediately. 'Don't argue with me, I'm not a fool like you!' He obeyed the orders and dared not to defend himself because arguing with Musebe would be fatal. He stood expressionless, staring at the reflection of himself in the well-polished surface of the table, awaiting his fate. Musebe was still counting for him his past sins, most of them imaginary and others simply products of office gossip, when the direct line on the table rang. He suspended Situma's case to pick the receiver.

'Hallo…yes, not bad dear… I'm just in the office… OK… Yes, I will be there shortly… But yesterday I waited for so long, what happened? Your phone was off, you could not be reached on either… OK … I'm coming bye…'

Musebe was a tall, dark, heavily built pot-bellied man, with a face full of wrinkles. He rarely smiled. He was ever gloomy, perhaps minding his own business, his face quite uninviting. But this morning after the phone conversation he smiled, a rare sign so far.

He wore black suits throughout the week and personally drove himself in his silver metallic Mercedes Benz. A great lover of women he was and his perceived social-economic influence made women fall for him easily. Competing with him over a woman was a sure way of inviting disaster. He could go to any length jostling for a woman he desired, even if it meant killing his rival.

Now, after the phone conversation, his moods turned jovial. A tinge of bright grin appeared on his face. He looked different and Situma could not help doubting if this was really the man who had been banging the table and reprimanding him furiously a moment ago. Long live the woman who rang, Situma blessed her. He then cleared a knot of phlegm from his throat and mumbled.

'Yesterday, Sir, I was mistakably picked up by the police… that's why I never turned up the rest of the day… I forgot my house keys here when I went back to collect this report and while I was breaking my door, the policemen mistook me for a robber.'

'So you slept in the cell?'

'No, I was released in the evening after they found me innocent.'

'But breaking doors is what thugs do, you cannot say they mistook you,' the boss responded rudely, unbothered. He looked at Situma with piercing eyes full of hatred and animosity. He did not believe the young man's explanation. He dismissed it as a mere tale. He clicked and laughed bossily because the previous evening, as he was meeting a friend in a city hotel, he spotted Situma and Nambozo in the same hotel chatting heartedly.

'Let me see your report,' he said passively without looking at Situma. He was busy drafting something in his notebook. Situma pushed it over to him across the table.

'I will call you later.' It was a statement.

Situma walked out of Musebe's office, marched past Nambozo at the reception and dashed into his office. He lit a cigarette and puffed smoke as he tried to imagine his fate. It was quite difficult to comprehend the measures likely to be taken by the big man. Everything here depended on the mood of the boss; a gloomy mood meant the sack and vice-versa.

It struck 12.45 p.m. Situma picked Nambozo from her desk and they went for lunch at Milembe Hotel. Again Musebe was here, seated under an umbrella with two ladies. He tilted his glasses and stared at his office secretary and the accountant.

'I wish we could have gone to another place away from this buffoon,' Situma whispered to Nambozo, but already spilt water could not be drawn back. It was too late to retreat. Musebe had caught them red handed, so to say.

'Forget about the old man; he has enough problems with his women. I wouldn't allow him to make advances at me and I made that clear to him. If anything, he has a daughter called Natasha who is my age or slightly older than me,' she said. Situma chuckled absent-minded.

After a hurried lunch, the two went back to the office leaving Musebe behind. That afternoon something disturbed Situma's mind so much; he looked worried, unsettled and confused. He was stressed. He struggled to compose himself and do some office work but to no avail. He continued brooding heavily about a host of nagging issues; the pending case with the boss and the disciplinary actions due, the lady he was determined to marry, Musebe's reaction to the news of their marriage and his supposed interference.

'Assuming all goes well and on the wedding day Musebe fires me, what shall I do?' he thought and shrank back. The extension line on his table rang and brought his mind back to the office. It was Musebe summoning him.

5

✦ ✦ ✦ ✦

The air had the stillness of death. Somewhere in a distance, Situma heard the noise of hooting vehicles at the bus park. He was seated outside his house contemplating how life was going to be; an uncertain today and possibly an empty tomorrow. He was nursing the anger of having been dismissed from the job, the way one caresses an aching tooth with the tip of the tongue to subdue the pain.

He remembered vividly how Musebe called him in the office that fateful afternoon and handed him a termination letter without much explanation. 'This organisation no longer requires your services…' the harsh letter read in part.

'Blessed is he who is accused falsely for the greatest is his reward in heaven,' Situma consoled himself with his father's popular phrase from the book of Mathew.

He retired to the house, banged the door behind him and slumped on the bed in a resigned and frustrated manner. His bed creaked under his weight. He tried to doze off from the frustrations and harsh realities of life but sleep could not come; not even a lull. He picked an old book, flipped through pages in a bid to divert his mind from his misfortunes but he could hardly concentrate. He just felt uneasy throughout the morning.

In the evening he met Watima at the famous Tepeka Club commonly known as *Meet Point*. Watima was a light-skinned, slender man who Situma shall forever remain thankful to for offering him accommodation as he looked for a job after a dramatic ejection from his uncle's house. He was in his late 20s and was a man of few words, best known to his friends as an action oriented man. His cool, handsome facade often made him pass for a harmless individual, perhaps a clergy-man.

However, he had a small scar on his cheek which he sus-tained many years ago when someone hit him with a bot-tle of beer in the bar after they had quarreled over a lady. He usually dressed in dark jeans and heavy cotton T-shirts unlike his friend Situma who donned suits. During his uni-versity days, Watima was on the forefront of disturbance whenever students rioted. He further exhibited his *comrade power* mentality through active participation in university politics; often teaming up with radical political activists for public protests. This eventually earned him an expulsion from Karoko University where he was studying a Bachelor of Science degree in Economics. He later joined a private uni-versity and completed his studies.

Now, Situma met him and they talked at length about the slippery nature of opportunities in life, how they come and go, how life is akin to a swinging pendulum (that has its highs and lows) and the need to soldier on despite the nasty roadblocks. Watima encouraged his friend to harden up say-ing 'life is full of ups and downs and to stumble is not to fall but rather to go ahead.'

It was month end and most people had loaded wallets and bulging pockets. Spending seemed not a problem at all. The pub was filled to capacity and many revellers were forced to look elsewhere. Every entrant looked different, smiles had replaced scowls and drinking had become some sort of a competition as drinkers placed their orders on large scale. Unlike other days when a patron could order for a single bottle of beer and sip quietly and for long, today the order was in large and generous quantities that even extended to the neighbouring tables.

'I have been sent to serve you with three bottles each from the man at the corner,' you could hear the waiter tell a group of about six people.

'Thank you, go and hug him on our behalf,' the excited recipients replied.

Meet Point, just like other pubs in the city, was a proclaimed 'fountain of wisdom' where people gathered for debates. Drinkers who were soccer fans talked about soccer. The famous European League had reached its climax and so they predicted the would-be champion. Politicians talked about politics of liberation and the impending general elections, the candidates, their suitability, their popularity and the political alliances that had been mooted to unseat the incumbent Prime Minister. Teachers talked of schools and the changes in the admission criteria, bankers talked of the high rates of inflation and how the shilling was performing against the dollar, and so on.

A police officer was also over-heard telling his colleagues how he squeezed a bribe of Sh. 500 from a motorist driving an unroadworthy vehicle. After all, they were at a social joint discussing and exchanging views pertaining to their professions. The next cop also talked of the harsh treatment he meted out on a chap who tried to rival him over a lady. 'I bundled him in the cells this morning, he will face charges related to drug trafficking.'

The bar at the same time was a cesspool of nonsense where cowards and fools got Dutch courage from the bottles in front of them and shouted at the top of their voices, making weird pronouncements.

A drinker who was a blacksmith by profession, known to his friends as Kongo, was heard commenting, 'These *wazungu* don't even know English. One of them came to my garage the other day and told me to weld his exhaust pipe. I was surprised but I had to do it for he wanted it done quickly and urgently. I instructed him to bend but he shouted 'not me, the vehicle!' From then I discovered that white men don't know English, no wonder they speak through their noses to hide their grammatical errors,' said Kongo as his drinking buddies exploded into a sensational laughter.

Situma could not laugh despite being within the hearing distance. The former Kentem accountant was deeply engrossed in thoughts, thinking of Nambozo and the job saga. Never had he met a lady so wonderful as Nambozo. He thought of how he was bound to lose her due to financial constraints and his heart sank. The glass he was holding accidentally fell off his grip and crashed on the hard floor. Watima stared at him blankly. Other people also turned their curious eyes in his direction.

'What is wrong *bwana*?' asked Watima. 'Why are you getting *high* so fast like this?'

'I'm not high, it's the…' Situma tried to say something about Nambozo but paused to summon courage and appropriate words to continue. Before he could resume speaking, Kongo shouted from the corner where he sat on a popular *sina tabu* stool. 'The sleepy monkey is drunk; take it home or else we shall have no glasses remaining in this pub.'

Watima got irritated, jumped over the table and went to grab Kongo, but he was restrained by the bouncers. 'You rogue, I can kill you! Bastard! You call my brother a sleeping monkey? Speak up again and I will square your round face.' Watima roared like a wounded lion.

He was known to attack his adversaries violently and beat them senseless. Had he not been restrained, he could easily send his adversary to the Intensive Care Unit. Kongo did not utter another word. His spell of drunkenness suddenly melted away, he kept still to himself and froze like water in an earthenware pot. He certainly sensed danger and regretted why he started all the mess by poking his nose into issues that did not concern him. He was known to be verbally unmatched but he dared not to throw a word back at Watima. Silently, he gulped his last beer and sneaked out of the bar through the rear exit.

The brief uproar caused some degree of argy-baggy commotion in the pub. After the unceremonious departure of Kongo, tension cooled off and a peaceful drinking atmosphere prevailed once more. Different views were, however, aired regarding the scene; people discussed Kongo's behaviour openly, terming it ungentleman. The patrons were progressively getting tipsy, holding their discussions in high tones; and the music too was booming loud.

The bar attendant came where Watima and Situma sat and the latter promised to pay cash for the broken glass.

'It's only Sh. 100,' he was told. Situma poured himself a drink, gulped and grimaced; the beer was tasteless and bitter. He hated it. Slowly but surely he started hating everything around him; the glass in front of him (he even though of hitting it on the floor again), the table where they sat, other drinkers, the waiters and even Watima himself. Nothing was interesting to Situma. He felt utterly desolate; life to him looked empty and disenchanting. He only wanted one person, Nambozo. Life could only be meaningful and complete with her.

His mind drifted back to Musebe who dismissed him unjustifiably. He remembered how Musebe called him in the office that afternoon, handed him a job termination letter without offering explanation and told him to vacate the office before the end of the day. Situma, however, blamed his sacking on his drinking habits; he accused himself for being careless and complacent on the job.

He also felt that Watima too was responsible for his dismissal! He argued that his recent outings with Watima made him overlook the preparation of the monthly report that conceived and eventually gave birth to the painful consequences he faced at work. He hated Watima and even felt like hurling a bottle of beer at him. Suddenly, he felt he could not enjoy being in the bar any longer, he just needed some respite away from any sort of noise, people's movements and the entire club hullabaloo. His hatred towards everything doubled and he regretted why he went to the pub.

Watima stood up, crossed the floor, reached an old juke-box machine (perhaps the only one still existing in town), pressed his favourite number, *Always* by the Atlantic Star, and came back to his seat. He then started singing with his girlfriend:

Girl you are to me
All that a woman should be
And I dedicate my love
To you… always

The song drove them into frenzy, and the couple could not help but stand up to dance as the rest of the drinkers cheered. A while ago the pub was tense when Watima almost fought with Kongo but now it was all happiness as people made merry. Situma stood up in a pin-drop silence and walked out without informing Watima. He did not wish to interfere with someone who had reached the climax of good times.

The outside air got him suddenly into its grip, making his skin prickle. A glare of streetlights made his head reel. He stood still to allow the spinning to subside. The spell of dizziness settled slowly in his head just like a merry-go-round and finally stopped. He had taken a lot of beer but the stress in him seemed to reduce the alcoholic effect. He crossed the streets and took the highway that led to his house. It was 10.30 p.m.

*   *   *

Situma was the first born in the family of five. Like other children from poor homes, he got his share of childhood diseases, joy and sorrows. His parents were keen on the growth of their son. They went through great pain; protecting their son from all manner of misfortunes in order to see him grow up into a healthy young man.

Wanami, a slender, bald-headed minister of God, made sure Situma received basic religious knowledge that would mould him into a God fearing son. He ensured his boy regularly attended Sunday school services. Whenever Situma complained of, say headache, stomachache or fever, his mother, Nandako, ran to all corners of the village in search of an antidote. However mild the bout was, she got struck with lots of worries.

For a growing boy like Situma, Nandako's overprotective hand was not always necessary. She had herself to blame one time when she showed her protective hand over Situma. It had rained in the afternoon and Situma joined his agemates for a skidding game down the river slope. At the age of 10, just like any other boy, childhood games were very popular among them hunting, hide and seek, storytelling and fishing. In the skidding game, Situma got into trouble when he wronged an older boy who was a bully. The bully hit him and a crying Situma went home to the consternation of the mother.

'What's up? Who did what?'

Amid sobs, the young Situma reported the incident and the offender to his mother. Nandako ran to where the children were playing. The bully was still there. She gave him a spanking that had him go home crying.

The drama that ensured later when the two protective mothers met was the best the boys had seen for days. Catcalls, jeers, name-calling and curses rent the air with each of the combatants ready to fight but not ready to begin the fight. The bully's mother, appearing enraged, took Nandako by surprise; she tripped her over into a heap. Nandako fell over with a heavy thud and the antagonist followed her down to the ground where they wrestled. The nasty village boys cheered save for Situma who shed tears of shame.

*   *   *

Situma started his primary education without a hitch. Joining the older boys and girls from the village, they walked the torturous five miles to school. This was a tiring and trying encounter especially for someone young like him. However the constant reminder from parents and teachers that the fruits of hard labour were sweet made the boys and girls endure the ordeal.

His progressive records showed a remarkable performance. He excelled in academics as well as extra-curricular activities, notably soccer. This earned him the recognition and respect that comes along with such achievements; he was made the headboy. Come the final exams, Situma performed well securing himself a place in one of the provincial secondary schools not far away from home.

Unlike his primary education, secondary was not so smooth. His parents could not easily raise fees and other levies. This made it difficult for him to learn uninterruptedly. His fees was occasionally raised from his uncles, the church and other well-wishers. However, when things worsened, he left school for a month or so, especially during planting and harvesting season to work with his parents and siblings in maize and coffee plantations to raise fees. Consequently, this was reflected in his classroom performance; it started taking a downward trend. Still, the sense of responsibility had been nurtured in the young Situma who, despite the hardships, took his studies seriously and managed to complete his secondary education with average grades.

After school, Situma spent time with his parents tending their two acre piece of land, their one cow and two sheep. He respected his parents who in turn only wished him well. He regularly got counsel from his parents and the church on how to handle life as a teenager. Appearing promising and eager to know more about God, and perhaps serve Him well like his father, Situma was appointed to the position of youth leader. It is believed that a lion begets a lion and like father like son; thus the church fraternity had great hopes that Situma would grow to assume his father's pastoral duties. The church kept discouraging him from bad influence: smoking, drinking and all kinds of vices, and always advised him to seek counsel from the Holy Bible.

'Take Jesus and the Bible as your shield in life. No enemy shall dare attack you… For it is written that if God is on our side, who can be against us!' said one of the brethrens who had visited Situma for a home fellowship.

As keen as Situma was to the counsel, there were times he could yield to peer pressure. Gambling, tumbling and crumbling along with life, he sometimes digressed but not much to cause alarm because it never got his parents' attention.

Two years later, after celebrating his 21ˢᵗ birthday, Situma was admitted to Karoko College to pursue a diploma course in accountancy. He got exposed to a new and civilised city environment; he acquired new friends, learnt new things and acquired new traits. Generally, he became a new person, a college guy. His mode of speech and even dressing changed.

One day, when he had come home at the end of the semester, he walked out in the company of his friends to meet other lost comrades. In the name of adventure and freedom to mingle, they went up to Kinambi town and joined other friends into a night club where they spent the night dancing, drinking and savouring the nocturnal life that night clubs offer. He returned home two days later with enough pack of lies to cover up the time out.

Convincing though, it raised eyebrows from his father Wanami for he had known his son not to go out on such a long trip, as alleged, without permission. However, the matter was rested without much fuss. But did Wanami know what Situma usually did with friends at college? Does he seek the Bible counsel anymore?

*   *   *

It was the tenth day of December and Christmas was only a few days away. Situma was resting in his apartment lost in thoughts, while listening to some Christmas carols playing from an FM radio station. The famous *Silent Night* was playing; its tune reflecting the cool and peaceful atmosphere of the festive season.

The presenter played another song – *Back to My Church*. The lyrics were so hypnotising and Situma could not help singing. The song was about deserting town life and joining people back in the hometown for a fellowship, never to come back to town again. What a timely message? What a coincidence? Moved by the song, Situma, for the first time since losing his job, strongly considered going back to his village, and stay.

A week later he boarded a Kinambi bound bus, 300 miles from the city. A large number of city residents were travelling upcountry for Christmas festivities and Situma happened to be part of the exodus. Due to the poor upcountry roads, the bus kept jerking passengers up and down. The old bus creaked and groaned along – like an oxen wagon – leaving behind a dark cloud of smoke.

'I doubt if we'll ever reach home. This junk of an automobile moves like a coal engine train! Maybe we'll reach Kinambi after an eternity,' he thought.

As it was his character, just like other civilised Karoko folks, he buried himself in a newspaper despite the regular jerks, rattling and deafening noise that emanated from the engine. Eventually, he got bored with the paper, folded it neatly, tucked it in his jacket pocket and sat pensively waiting for the end of his journey. He had nobody to converse with; he knew none of the people on the bus and did not wish to know any. He was not a happy man and was not in the mood of conversation. He thought of how he would approach his parents over his sacking.

'I will tell papa that Musebe hates me for no apparent reasons...' he thought and froze back to assess the genuineness

and the weight that this excuse carried. 'No, I won't tell him that,' he tried to plan another somehow valid and believable tale. He dozed off in the process only to wake up and find that they had already reached Kinambi town. How fast! He had been sleeping for the last three hours!

He searched for his bag that contained his clothes and some personal effects but it was missing. It had been stolen. He reported the matter to the bus conductor and his driver but they were not helpful. Instead of promising some compensation or anything to do with that, a rude conductor showed him a sticker pined at the exit door which read: *Chunga mizigo yako mwenyewe*, translated as goods are carried at the owner's risk.

'Were you not sleeping when some boys alighted at Bombori with a lot of luggage? How could I know that yours was among them? Wake up to this world, man!' the conductor retorted.

After a heated argument with the bus crew whom he accused of conspiracy to rob him, Situma left the bus park so annoyed and went his way home empty handed, save for a newspaper he carried.

While crammed in a fourteen-seater *matatu* heading to his home village, but now carrying over 20 passengers, Situma planned how to open a conversation with his people but it seemed so absurd to plan for so vague a scene that he was headed to stage at home. How tasteless and careless will it look if I reveal to them that I was fired for negligence of duty? He found himself shrinking inexpressively.

It was on a Saturday evening and every family member was at home preparing to attend tomorrow's Sunday service that always took the whole day. Unlike in the town set-up where people attended mass for only two hours or even less, here, Sunday was fully dedicated to God and church affairs. The service usually began at around 10 a.m., depending on the available quorum, and ended slightly past 4.00 p.m. The order of service included receiving greetings from sister churches, several choir performances from the youth, women and elders, testimonies from members (with no time limit imposed), a sermon to welcome the preacher, the main sermon from the preacher and finally, a long list of announcements. So family members were at home ironing their 'Sunday best' clothes using a charcoal iron-box.

Despite the general level of poverty that prevailed at home, there was slaughtering of a goat that reinforced a small homecoming into a big party that attracted the neighbours who streamed Wanami's home in the name of friends, brothers, sisters and cousins to greet Situma.

Situma, who mainly used to put on black cotton suits, seemed to be in a wrong place. He exhibited a great economic gap between him and the rest of the family members. The tattered clothes worn by the father, mother and siblings portrayed deep-rooted poverty in their home.

As a peasant farmer, Wanami had no stable source of income other than five or slightly more bags of maize that he sold to middlemen at the end of every harvesting season. The government cereals board only accepted maize from farmers in bulk. Wanami could, therefore, not afford fashionable clothing for his children and himself. But as Nandako said, 'Happiness is far much better than wealth and a good name is better chosen than immense riches.' So this evening, she was extremely happy to see her son again and she engaged him in an endless conversation on various livelihood topics.

With her in-born characteristic anxiety, she posed endless questions to Situma about his life in the city and how he was coping with it. 'But it's high time you got a partner… you know…somebody to take care of you and your household. Remember we need grannies too,' she suggested marriage to her son. Situma welcomed the idea and promised to 'do something about it soon.'

Wanami also seemed to have much interest in Situma's well being but not like Nandako. He looked forward to his son's marriage but was not ready to urge him on, as was the mother. The old man chose an easy topic. He talked about politics a little bit, the general welfare at home and the regular bouts of sickness, hunger and the continued dry spell that had consequently affected crops and the health of his two animals.

Wanami had five children. The first-born, Situma, was twenty-six. Waliaula, the second born aged twenty-three was, a student in a Teachers Training College (TTC). His education was sponsored by Namufweli Friends Church. The third born, Gladys, nineteen, was a form four student at Kinambi High School. A form two student in the same school, Catherine, was sixteen. The last-born, Fred Wamela was ten. This is the boy Wanami loved so much right from birth. Father's love was evident when the old man took the little boy with him wherever he went, even on long trips.

Come Sunday, the small boy carried his father's Bible bag to and from church. Fred showed much interest in knowing the word of God and his father promptly devoted his energies to ensure he got all the basic religious knowledge. During his free time, he taught Fred how to pray and some basic divinity doctrines based on Biblical stories. Among Wanami's best stories for Fred was the prodigal son, the battle between the minion David and the mighty Goliath and the feeding of 5,000 hungry people by Jesus.

Now, when Wanami asked Situma about the job and how he was finding it, Situma answered casually, 'It's just fine dad, I'm pushing along well.' He hated to be asked this question that he was completely avoiding. He did not wish to hear anything about his job mentioned, let alone discussed.

'Hold on tight Situma, make sure you don't lose your good job. Nowadays getting employment is like mining gold!' said Wanami and continued, 'You are one of the luckiest sons from this low-land region to land a nice job in the city. Our community is proud of you… And no doubt Karoko climate had favoured you greatly. You've changed drastically for the last three years, today you have added weight, your skin is lighter and I can notice many other positive changes too,' the old man spoke with a face denoting total happiness. To Situma, his father's words were a tinge of irony especially when he insisted on holding tight on the job. *'Maybe someone leaked the information that I was sacked and so they are laying a trap to test my sincerity,'* Situma thought.

'Oh God is great,' concluded Wanami and asked the family members to bow down for a prayer and thank the Almighty for showering blessings onto their son.

He started praying, praising the Lord and thanking Him because of Situma. Deeply engrossed in thoughts, with his head bend low, his eyes not closed, Situma did not hear the rest of the prayer but 'Amen' jolted his mind back in the house. He felt like breaking the sad news (about his dismissal) to them but something stopped him; telling them such ungodly news at such a heavenly hour would be more of an insult.

That night he lay awake trying to picture his parents' response in case he revealed to them he was jobless. Will dad continue praising the Lord? Won't mum rip herself apart and wail throughout the village? Oh, no, I should continue keeping them in darkness for some time…for happiness' sake. Still his guilty conscience darted over the lie. This deprived him of sleep. Many questions came into his mind and faded back unattended to. He tried to get an indirect way of breaking the sad news to his parents but none seemed appropriate. He arrived to a conclusion of going back to the city and write them a letter or send someone to inform them. It was 2.00 a.m. when he finally fell asleep.

He woke up late with a hagridden and visibly troubled face; he looked tired and bored stiff, yawning regularly and staring blankly into space. Breakfast was served but he had no appetite. He only took a cup of black tea for the sake of it, to avoid many questions from his mother about his sudden lack of appetite.

'I have to leave you dad,' he announced after breakfast. 'I was only given a short break of two days, yesterday and today. I have to report back to work tomorrow morning.'

'I wish you stayed longer my son so that you meet and greet some members of our church,' the old man regretted.

'That was my wish too, but the strict working conditions at Kentem can't allow me to stay out any longer, despite the festive season having started. I wish I was in government employment where one easily gets a leave. For your information, this week, I will be travelling with our manager for a business trip in the neighbouring country. They intend to open another branch there soon, so we're going to survey the area. I would have really wished to be with you for Christmas. It's long since I attended service with members of our church,' said Situma.

'Anyway, travel safely and communicate regularly,' said Wanami.

'And you appear tired and rather bored… what's wrong Situma? Did you sleep well?' asked Nandako, always ready to stand by his son for better or worse and ever keen on every detail.

'Yah, I slept pretty well mum,' Situma said and forced a grin. Nandako appeared as if she wanted to add something but Wanami cut her short to say a prayer.

'Okay then travel safely and may the Lord guide you till you reach the city,' she said after a farewell remark.

6

◆ ◆ ◆ ◆

Wandering up and down the streets of Karoko City, Situma decided to check on Watima and get the latest updates. The last time they saw each other was almost a month ago in the bar where Watima almost roughed up Kongo for abusing him. He went to Miami Financial Scheme where Watima worked as an accountant and found him busy in the office.

'Hi Situma, welcome… have a seat,' Watima hugged his friend and ushered him onto a settee. He was busy on the computer but the appearance of Situma made him suspend the work he was doing. 'You're lost I must say, I have not seen you in town of late. I even developed a feeling the boys in blue might have picked you up for…' Watima commented jokingly.

'I had just gone home for hibernation but the cave was so cold, prompting me to resurface,' Situma said of his trip home. They all laughed at the well-crafted metaphorical statement.

'Any development? You look very smart, you must be doing something somewhere, I guess,' Watima observed.

'Not yet, I'm still in the dark. The other day I sent a job application letter to Shell Company and Ramuti Investments but I'm still waiting for whatever response they will send me. You never know, it can be positive or regrets.'

'I came to see you in your house recently but found your door shut with a big padlock. Your neighbours said you had not been seen around for some time. I met Nambozo in town but she had no useful information either. None of us knew anything on your whereabouts… that's why I was apparently right to think of looking for you all over the police stations, just in case…'

'Eer Watima, you can't say anything without mentioning the police? Don't remind me of those cantankerous fellows, the public enemies who enjoy seeing people suffer,' said Situma, 'You know what? Let me tell you something… I once visited my cousin, a police constable at Kinambi police station and didn't find him in the station. I was told to wait for he had gone on a security operation and was expected back in a short time. So I rested on a bench near the OCS's office waiting for him. Within a short while, a police landrover full of suspects pulled into the station.

'Was it recently?' Last week?' Watima cut in.

'No this happened several years ago when I was still in college. So, as I was saying, the landrover came with a bundle of suspects and I spotted my cousin in the front seat. He didn't see me. He alighted and rushed quickly to another office on the opposite block across the parking bay.

'I stood up and followed him over. One police officer who was pacing back and forth within the station ordered me to go back. 'Hey go back!' were his words. I thought the place I was heading to was out of bound for civilians, so I went back where I was seated before. The idiot followed me and repeated his words loud and clear '*kijana* go back where others are!' I could not understand him. I kindly begged him to explain what he meant while at the same time telling him the reason why I had visited the station, but he could hardly listen to me.

'He dragged me forcefully, slapped me on the face and frog-matched me into the remand house where others were. He then spoke to his colleague in some rugged Kiswahili '*Haka ni kamkora kalikuwa kanajaribu kutoroka. Hebu kapee brush ya mgongo kwanza.*' The other fellow received the orders and worked on my back with the bamboo cane mercilessly.'

'Gosh! What a fate worse than death? Is that the meaning of conducting investigations and serving the people?' Watima observed rhetorically. Situma continued narrating the ordeal about his fateful visit.

'At around 8.00 p.m., three cops came in to do some manual work: routine clobbering of suspects as they called it, and they were all drunk. Luckily, my cousin was among the three terrorists. Brandishing their flexible canes, they set on the suspects whipping them terribly and recklessly–on the back, head, legs and anywhere. I called out his name and he noticed me among the inmates. He was stunned, I could see it. 'How did you get here *wandase?* Were you among the arsonists we brought in this evening?'

'I explained the events that led to my arrest and boldly, with passionate hate, pointed an accusing finger at the cop who dragged me in the remand cell. After brief consultations, I was released unconditionally. Since then, I hardly visit a police station, maybe only when I'm under arrest. Besides that, I hate police officers with a passion.'

Watima shook his head amazed. He was amazed by Situma's story. The incident was saddening and amusing too. He didn't know whether to laugh at Situma or pity him. But before he could say anything, Situma added, 'I was ordered to remove my shoes and other documents I had on me; money, National ID, everything. I was only given back my ID when they released me. The money disappeared and so did my pair of shoes.'

'And what of last week?' Watima asked with an intention of changing the topic so that he could tell his friend the good news he had for him.

'Last week I just went home, Kinambi.'

'It's good you're back. I'm glad to see you. There is a job opportunity available somewhere and I want you to take it. You qualify for it,' said Watima.

'Where?' the anxious job seeker was eager to know more.

'Here,' Watima pointed at the desk next to him. 'You see I'm alone in this office. The other desk is vacant. The occupant left us. He resigned and his position has been advertised.'

'Look at the bugger...why did he quit?'

'Maybe he's got some greener pastures elsewhere,' lied Watima. He did not wish to reveal that Harun had been fired for refusing to be an accomplice in a fraudulent deal in which their boss was involved. The Miami boss had wanted the two to be his henchmen in signing and approving the purchase of items that were never delivered. Harun refused to co-operate and next came a termination letter alleging neglect of duty. Prior to his dismissal, Harun had travelled upcountry for the burial of his relative when the boss declared he had absconded duty and fired him, the oral permission he had given him earlier notwithstanding.

Situma received news of the vacant position in the company with lots of relief. He could not help jumping on his feet with joy when he saw renewed hope in his job hunting ventures. Miami Limited boss was Watima's maternal uncle. This, Situma was sure, could help oil wheels for easier movements. He pulled Watima closer and begged him, 'Please, my friend, I'm desperate. Tell your uncle to give me this position. Please lobby for me. Tell him all the good things you know about me.' Watima promised to do his best.

It got to 1.00 p.m. They went out for lunch and then Situma proceeded to Marai to bring his certificates and other credentials. He availed them to Watima the same afternoon, having already written a cover letter and a curriculum vitae.

They parted ways and agreed to meet in the evening at *Meet Point* to 'mark the register.' Situma went back to his apartment and opted not to join Watima that evening because he had no money to buy beer and he did not wish to just sit around as his friends settled all the bills.

Having foregone the drinking spree, he relaxed in his house reading a motivational book *Help me, I'm Alone* written by an American female televangelist. He was deeply engrossed in the book when he heard a slight tap on his door at around 8.00 p.m. He believed that it was Watima looking for him.

'Get in comrade but I'm not in the mood of going out as agreed,' he said as he stood up to open the door. After setting it ajar, the person he saw gave him a pleasant surprise.

'Oh sweetie, welcome' he hugged his visitor, Nambozo. She sat on the bed and Situma sat next to her. 'I've missed you dear,' he told her.

'Me too, though you currently behave as if your departure from Kentem meant departure from me also,' she said as she stole a glance at him to see his reaction. Situma just chuckled. She however persisted, 'I guess you've got some chic somewhere…'

'No, Nambozo, I can't leave you, my one and only,' he assured her. They held hands and looked at each other in the eyes. Situma then asked her: 'Nambozo, do you really wish to be with me, stay with me, forever?' She just looked at him as if she did not understand what he actually meant.

Situma rephrased his question, 'Do you take Situma to be your lawfully wedded husband, to love, to cherish and to hold?'

'Yes, I do,' she said.

*   *   *

A week had elapsed and Watima had not communicated to Situma about the progress of the job deal at Miami Financial Scheme. Just like any other job seeker in the world, he was anxious to know whether plans to employ him at Miami were on course.

'May I speak to Mr. James Watima, Finance Department?' he said courteously to the lady at the reception.

'Do you want to see him on official or private matter?'

'Private.'

'May I know where you come from, please?'

'From Mukhweya Holdings,' Situma gave a fictitious address.

'I'm sorry he is not around now, try later.'

'OK I will come back in the afternoon. Tell him Situma was here.'

'I will,' she said and smiled at him. Situma looked at her and acknowledged her beauty, she is lovely, he concluded.

As Situma went out, he regretted why he did not ask for the receptionists name and possibly, her contacts. Going back could look odd, so he rued his missed opportunity and proceeded on.

While walking along the city streets, his mind switched to Nambozo. The memory of their last meeting came alive and vivid; what a wonderful moment with the goddess of love. The thirst of seeing her struck him again. He reached the nearest booth and dialed her office number. After a hearty conversation he fixed a lunch date at Milembe Hotel.

The city clock struck 1.00 p.m. The flow of human traffic in the streets going out for lunch was incessant. Situma crossed the jammed streets and found his way to the hotel where he sat in a secluded corner and ordered a soda. Most entrants came in pairs – a lady and a man. This made him feel out of place but he was sure his lady would eventually join him and he would no longer look the odd one out.

In the meantime he kept himself busy with a newspaper, catching up with daily news and reading the opinions of his favourite columnists, especially political commentaries.

Thirty minutes gone, Nambozo had not turned up. An hour later, still she had not appeared. He had by now read the whole newspaper; local news, international news, business, sports and even classified advertisements. The bottle of soda in front of him appeared more of a decoration on the table. He hardly touched it. So far, he had only sipped his drink twice in an hour's time.

Situma, lately worried that his relationship with Nambozo was bound to collapse due to financial constraints, started suspecting that she had been taken out for lunch by some big monied competitor, or even Musebe himself.

'I was his main obstacle, he sacked me and I believe he has now taken her,' he reflected. The thought of Musebe finally winning the heart of Nambozo disturbed Situma. He sat musing over his lone bottle of soda wondering the next move to take now that Nambozo had proved to be 'unreliable and untrustworthy.'

He remembered the receptionist at Miami. *I wish I had her contacts, I would invite her for lunch instead,* he regretted. He was almost giving up, standing up to leave the place when Nambozo finally appeared. Amid a conglomeration of eyes feasting on her, she crossed the floor to where Situma sat and apologised for coming late.

'I've been here from 1.00 p.m.,' he said without betraying the bitter feelings in him. She looked at her watch, 2.15 p.m.

'Sorry for keeping you that long. I'm from St. Cecilia Hospital. Cynthia is sick…terrible fever…I got a call from her teacher and I had to rush and take her for treatment. She is now responding well at least…thanks for your patience…I thought I could not find you here…' And so was the endless trail of excuses.

Just like the morning sun rises and clears away all the mist off the face of the earth, making it dry and serene, so did the negative thoughts that Situma had developed about her got washed away. The two chatted casually, discussing and cursing Musebe. Situma, while praising himself as usual, something he was fond of doing before ladies, lied that he had already secured a job with Miami Financial Scheme.

'I told you I'm marketable. The other day the Manager of Miami called me to his office for an informal chat and he hired me immediately. I tell you many people are in need of my services. And here they pay better than Kentem; I now earn money…eh, not peanuts like what Musebe used to offer me.'

'Don't tell me that! You mean you are now in the same office with Watima?' she asked, excited.

'Exactly, that is it. In fact, Watima and I are just inseparable.'

Situma then told her his plans. 'I want to take you home, to Kinambi, to meet my parents, then we shall also visit your family… and thereafter we will wed,' he said with lots of certitude. The tone of his speech was what could be described as a sure one. He even quoted a familiar bible verse:

For one shall live his parents, join his wife
And they will no longer be two, but one body…
And what God has joined
No man shall put asunder.

The two placed their order for lunch and talked at length about their future plans as a married couple. That afternoon, Nambozo did not report back to work. She just wanted to be with Situma and have the whole of him for herself. She had strongly fallen in love and parting with him seemed painful.

She felt great, loved and envisioned a happy life with Situma ahead. Unlike other ladies who are often jilted and mistreated in relationships, Nambozo felt her majesty Eros had blessed her with a fine gentleman who would make her dreams come true.

'Situma, I never knew what love was until I met you,' she confessed.

*   *   *

Situma walked into Miami offices the following morning and unlike other days, the place was quiet but busy. He went to the counter and stretched his hand to greet the reception-ist. Yes, her palm was very soft, he liked it. He thought of holding it longer, but no, he had to let it go.

'You forgot to tell me one thing yesterday when I was here,' he said.

'What could that be?' she anxiously paid attention.

'Your name,' Situma said almost in a whisper.

'Call me Irene,' she said.

'You know the meaning of Irene?' he asked. She shook her head sideways in negation and asked him to tell her the meaning instead.

'It means the *good one*…' Situma said and they both laughed but she was cautious not to be drawn into a moving bandwagon.

'Anyway, is Watima around?'

'No,' she said and informed him of the changes that had taken place in the company. Situma learnt that Watima and his uncle-cum-boss had been arrested by the anti-corruption unit for allegedly swindling the company over Sh. 5 million.

'I can't believe my ears, five million shillings stolen?'

'Yes, that is according to the auditors who perused through the books of accounts the other day,' said Irene.

Situma pitied his comrade. He remembered his last conversation with Watima. The latter had hinted to him of a deal he was working on; a deal to instant riches. Watima had talked of buying a house in the city and a car, preferably a Mercedes. Is this the deal he meant? He pitied his friend. I wish I could do something to bail him out. If only I had money to engage a top lawyer. *'Oh, poor James…Why you?'*

Now, where do I begin? This unfortunate occurrence has dealt a deathblow to my endeavours. Who will help me get a job here? But disparity is a fool's consolation. I'm not a fool, so I can't despair… Forward Situma! I will traverse across barriers, hills and valleys until I reach my destiny.

'So Watima is in police custody?'

'That's it…'

'Which station?'

'It has been kept a secret, even from us, as further investigations are still underway. Nobody is allowed to visit the suspects or even know where they're being held,' said Irene.

'So, how do interested parties get to know the progress of their case? Which number should I call in case I want to know more about Watima's fate?'

'But he is no longer here, his services have been terminated, how can we help you sincerely?' she asked.

'It's your organisation that has accused him of theft and if anything you should know how the case concerning the offender and your money progresses.'

'Then call this office for an update,' she said and gave him the office number.

'I suppose when I call this number you will be the one to receive and I hope you can't deny me any information… I'm worried some other fellow may hung up on me and deny me information about my long time pal.'

'If information is for the public then the public will be told,' she said, 'or alternatively let me give you more contacts.' She wrote down two more numbers and labelled them 'mobile.'

'Thank you for your concern. Have a nice time Irene. I will call you.'

'You are welcome, Situma,' she said as he took to the exit.

'Now, I have her contacts. I will tell her my feelings.'

The manager who took over from Watima's uncle advertised Watima's position and even went ahead to re-instate the sacked Harun. Situma was advised to apply for the job too. His application letter was the first to be received. The new manager looked at his school and college certificates, the CV and other credentials and termed them rich. They called him for an interview.

'And why did Kentem Limited lay off such a highly qualified and experienced worker?' the manager wondered. He decided to call them to ascertain something. He dialed Musebe's direct line.

'Kentem Limited, can I help you?

'Yes, may I speak to the manager?'

'Speaking, go ahead.'

'Now, do you know Mr Situma Wanami, formally an employee in your organisation, Finance Department?'

'Of course, I know that scoundrel.'

'Scoundrel! How? What do you mean... er...why was he laid off? And how was his general performance, anyway? He embezzled company funds?'

'He as well as did it... he was one of the laziest workers that Kentem has ever had. After constant warning and no improvement, we fired him due to negligence of duty and inefficiency. He can only work under tight supervision,' Musebe literally hammered the last nail on Situma's coffin.

'Hello.'

'Yes, I can hear you.'

'What's your personal advice, we are planning to recruit him in our organisation.'

'Go ahead and employ him at your own risk,' said Musebe.

The Miami Manager informed the interviewing panel about his conversation with Musebe and they unanimously resolved to drop Situma's name.

Situma entered virtually every office in the city looking for employment but luck was not with him. Wherever he presented himself, he was turned back and sometimes given promises that were never fulfilled. He read newspapers daily, checking the job vacancies column and wrote numerous job applications but all proved unsuccessful.

Situma was an extravagant spender; he had not saved a cent for the rainy season. He was outstanding in making the budget for savings and expenditure of company funds but he never made a budget of his own salary. He operated a bank account for the sole purpose of receiving his salary but not saving. He failed to pay rent for his house in Marai for two months and was kicked out by the landlord. Most of his valuable property was seized to act as security for the arrears. The landlord put a big padlock on the door.

That night Situma came back with hired thugs, captured the watchman at gunpoint, broke into the house, *stole* his own property, made the watchman to load them onto a pick up, drove off with him and abandoned him in a bush, helpless. Good Samaritans rescued the guard in the morning. The landlord found an empty house with Situma having escaped to another part of the city. He had actually stolen his own property this time round! He relocated to the lower class residential area, Bondeni, where he rented a single room for Sh. 500 per month as compared to Sh. 5,000 that he used to pay at Marai.

The landlord, accompanied by police, went to Kentem Ltd offices and talked to Musebe about the incident, which they termed as robbery. They hoped to find Situma there and bring him to justice, but he had been fired several months earlier.

Life in Bondeni was not easy for Situma. Electricity, piped water and other social amenities were not available here. Occasionally, he had to go as far as 2 kilometres away from where he stayed to draw water from a public borehole. This happened when he could not afford water from the hawkers who sold a 20-litre container at Sh. 20.

Now a jobless and frustrated man, he resorted to taking local beer, *malwa* and *chang'aa,* because he could not afford bottled beer. And if ever he happened to eat at least one meal a day, he counted himself lucky. He had slumped into a state where eating two meals a day appeared luxurious. This hard lifestyle compelled him to sell most of his household items for survival. He sold the gas cooker, the sofa set, the TV, and other items at a throw away price. He basically disposed them because he was broke and he needed money to survive, and two, there was nowhere to keep them. The multipurpose room that he lived in was too small.

After a transaction, Situma assumed his former high-class lifestyle and started drinking as never before. He went to the bar as early as 10.00 a.m. and could spend the whole day dinking. As it was common with him, he bought beer for his friends and even strangers with profound intention of showing off his wealth.

Occasionally the people he treated to brands of Whisky, Guinness, ESB, Tusker, Pilsner, Nile Special, Chairman and all other labels from the brewers, looked at him with scorn as a misguided individual. Others gave him false and dry praises aimed at milking him dry. And whenever the happy-go-lucky Situma met with his acquaintances, he told them that he was a businessman.

'I left Kentem because I prefer running my own enterprise to serving other people and gaining little or nothing at the end. In fact, I got a tender to supply gold and silver to some firms that manufacture jewelry in town. It's really lucrative!' he often said.

He even once implored his friend who worked for a publishing company as a sales executive to resign from the slavery jobs of distributing books and join him in business ventures. 'I'll strike a deal with my colleagues so that we initiate you into our organisation.' But where and when did he carry out such?

With the money he had, Situma took Nambozo to executive places for treats. They attended discos every weekend and visited all entertainment spots in town. This period, he enjoyed life with his lover to their best. More often than not, he booked a hotel in town where they spent the night. He dared not take her to his single room in Bondeni slums, leave alone mention to her that he resided there. He couldn't make such a mistake and the issue of his place of residence suddenly became top secret.

*　　　*　　　*

One evening, Situma dialed Nambozo's mobile number so that they could meet in town for dinner. 'The subscriber of the number you have dialed cannot be reached,' came the response. He got annoyed and he wondered why Nambozo was fond of switching off her phone. Situma had always been preaching to his friends about the disadvantages of having one lover.

'You know ladies are unpredictable; men with single lovers usually get frustrated but those who have multiple girlfriends will never be let down. If one fails to co-operate, you simply walk over to the next. If one is not available, you try the next.' Thus, he decided to call Irene, and the call went through, yes, she was available.

'Hello, Irene, this is Situma.'

'Oh… Situma, long time, what's up?'

'Business, I'm too busy to even pick a phone call. As I had told you before, my business calls for total attention. Last week I was outside the country meeting my business associates.'

'So what's new Mr Busyman?'

'Let us meet at Nandos for dinner, in thirty minutes' time, please. That's when we'll talk more.'

When Situma arrived at Nandos, Irene was already there, seated. She stood up and hugged him passionately. She was clad in a red dress and a black top. Dinner was served, chicken, potato chips and other sumptuous accompaniments. A bottle of wine crowned it all as they toasted for the continuity of their love–which had started secretly–with Irene playing second fiddle to Nambozo. As usual, Situma assured Irene that she was the woman of his dreams, and she, in return, took him seriously as her Mr Right.

'I came to work in the city three months ago under protest. I wanted to join a university abroad and study Communication and Media but things got complicated the last minute. My dad then decided to hook me up with a friend who found me a job here, hardly did I know that it was a blessing in disguise…so that I meet you dear…' she said happily.

'It's nice to hear that my dear, soon we'll wed and live together until death separates us.'

'It's my wish to live and see that dream come true,' she said as Situma pecked her on the cheek. They drank late into the night until she could no longer see or walk. She leaned on Situma's lap and dozed. Situma booked a room where they savoured the rest of the night.

*　　　*　　　*

Elsewhere, Nambozo discovered she was pregnant and wished to inform Situma of the new development; to give him good news that soon he would be a father. She tried to contact him at Miami and inform him about the issue, and urge him to speed up their wedding arrangements but he was not there. The truth now dawned on her; Situma did not work with Miami and had never worked there before. *'He must have lied to me,'* she concluded and wept bitterly. The idea of abortion crossed her mind but she quickly rejected it.

7

◆ ◆ ◆ ◆

Situma was strolling in the slums of Bondeni when he came across a cart puller. He stopped him, posing as a customer. On a friendly note he enquired about the profitability of *mkokoteni* business, as the local people called it. Wambete, the cart puller, explained to him that the business paid well, but only the fittest could survive. The work involved transporting goods for traders from the market place to their respective destinations or carting goods for shoppers from hardwares, supermarkets, among others.

Having resolved to do any job available, regardless of its nature, as long as it enabled him to put food on the table, Situma told him that he was ready for the job. Through a verbal agreement he entered into a partnership with Wambete after paying some 'incorporation fee.'

Due to the economic hardship he had fallen into, Situma had no option but to venture into the *mkokoteni* business. At the start, the initiative earned him some money and he could at least afford the 'luxury' of eating two meals a day. Nevertheless, this was a demanding venture; one was supposed to be physically fit. Such demand, coupled with some aspects of despair, pushed Situma into the culture of abusing drugs.

This changed Situma's behaviour and general way of thinking; he changed from a cautious, positive thinking individual who grew up in a religious home to a reckless and hopeless man with negative thoughts of a vagabond brought up in the streets. His perception of the world changed from a place where people co-habit amicably and help each other whenever in need to a jungle where animals compete for survival through exercising muscle power, and preying on each other.

Wambete was a feared man owing to his character and physical appearance. He wore dreadlocks and had bloodshot eyes. Despite his young age – just in late 20s – his face was terribly wrinkled owing to his hard lifestyle. He had once been jailed for three years for robbery with violence.

During the day, he pulled his cart as usual and at night, he turned to robbery. He owned a pistol which he stole from a policeman who got drunk and dozed off in a bar. This *empty tool*, as he called it, acted merely as a scarecrow, for it had no bullets. And he managed to rob even motorists using it.

Situma, with a strong thought of 'people-fit-into-situations-but-not-situations-into-people' gradually shaped hi-mself to fit in this new lifestyle. Job is job, he muttered to himself whenever he saw someone staring at him. There was nobody around to console him and he chose to console himself. *'Where is Nambozo? What about the lovely Irene?'* He thought about them and regretted why he severed communication links with his girlfriends. He was never proud of the circumstances that life had pushed him into and could not allow them to discover the kind of life he currently led. It was a dog's life.

*   *   *

It was yet another December. A year had passed since Situma was last seen at home. Wanami, a caring and responsible father who wanted to see the continuity of his family tree, had engaged a girl for his son to marry. Nekoye, the chosen bride, was the daughter of Milimo, also a Quakers Church elder.

'As for me and my house we shall serve the Lord.' That was the message that stood bold, firm and distinct on the wall of Wanami's living room. He had chosen to dedicate his life to serving God; and that is exactly what everyone knew him for.

'Pastor' was his name. Besides preaching in church every Sunday, he mobilised other brothers and sisters within his mission for house-to-house fellowship. That Thursday evening the faithful were gathered in his house to meditate upon the word of God. They had made a weekly merry-go round system where fellowships were conducted in different houses. As routine, a cup of tea accompanied the service, but members were careful to ensure the word of God received paramount attention while earthly desires such as food came second.

'Praise the Lord brothers and sisters,' Wanami called out and the gathering of about a dozen believers responded with a resounding 'Amen.'

'The Bible says that whenever two or three are gathered in His name, the presence of the Lord is guaranteed. As we gather here to meditate upon His word, we believe that He is here with us…for us…hallelujah!'

'Amen,' the answer came full and alive.

'Brothers and sisters, the gates of heaven are narrow – one has to struggle to go through. However, the gates of hell are so wide – effort is required to get there. You just glide over. The kingdom of heaven suffereth violence and the violent take it by force… We are currently living in a dirty society, the Sodom and Gomorrah type. This world is no longer the good place that God originally intended it to be. People are focused on competing each other in thinking evil and acting evil. Our sons and daughters, the people who were once the pride of parents, have turned into rogues that bring shame back home. The rate at which drug addiction and prostitution is practised amongst our youth is alarming. We want to pray and intercede over this matter and ask God to unshackle his children from the yoke of the devil… praise the Lord?'

'Amen.'

'Besides that, we want to pray for peace and stability in our country. Let there be no tribal clashes in our nation. May people learn to live together as children of God regardless of their cultural backgrounds. Corruption has become the order of the day in our country. People attend church services in large numbers but do not follow the commandments of God. That is not the way God wants it to be. We should be more of good doers of the word than just mere listeners… lest when the Day of Judgment comes, we shall be scoffed at: 'Get away from me you workers of iniquity; I don't know you.'

'And as Christians, we have the moral duty to intercede for our nation and ensure the word of God reaches all those in darkness because it is written: 'go ye unto the world and make disciples of all nations.' The scripture further says that knock and the door shall be opened, seek and thou shall find, ask and it shall be given…We have to pray ceaselessly until our prayers are answered…hallelujah!'

'Amen!'

'But before we pray, it is my humble pleasure to invite brother Milimo to give us a brief sermon. *Karibu sana ndugu.*'

Milimo talked about taming the tongue because it is small but a lethal organ. 'It is like a matchstick that can set ablaze the entire forest, but if well tamed, the tongue can bring great development.' In his closing remarks, he touched on children as a blessing from God. He applauded the missionaries for spreading the word of God far and wide to all nations scattered all over but sharply attacked them for what he called intoxicating the mind of African youth with a culture they could not understand or fit in.

As he concluded, he thanked God for blessing Wanami with children who had all along resisted the temptations of being lured into youthful, destructive, worldly pleasures. He singled out Situma as an example of an obedient and focused child who always walked in the ways of the Lord.

When the evening fellowship came to an end, Wanami told the faithful about his impending trip to Karoko City to visit his son but did not divulge the purpose of his visit. He simply said he wanted to 'find out how his son was faring on with life in a far away land.' He earnestly requested for prayers as he travelled to the city.

Wanami and Nandako had for long been looking forward to the wedding of their son. According to them, this ceremony was long overdue. So they felt they had the moral duty to help their son put some things in place, especially marriage matters. They decided to travel to the city and deliver to Situma the good news about Nekoye.

They left Namufweli at 4.00 a.m. using the earliest bus and by 12.00 p.m., they were already in the city. As true village folks, they were dressed casually and this made them look out of place in the city. Nandako had malwoven pieces of *khangas* wrapped around her body and she was barefooted. She had borrowed a pair of shoes from her neighbour for the trip but they pinched her until she removed and kept them in her bag. Her feet were not used to shoes.

Wanami wore an ill-knotted tie and a second hand coat that had creases all over, especially after the long and bumpy ride across the country's dusty roads. He wore a faded trouser that had several patches around the knees. His shoes were bent on one side; the sole having been repaired over and over. For a village pastor, this was very admirable.

This was Nandako's first trip to the city. She stared at everybody and everything. From the skyscrapers to the neatly trimmed street lawns; things looked marvellous. She wondered how a fleet of vehicles could follow each other closely in a long convoy within the city without knocking each other. Everything to her appeared extra-ordinary.

Wanami had a map of Situma's estate so they used it to trace him. They got to Marai and knocked on the door number 605, the house that formally belonged to Situma. They did not know that their son had shifted to Bondeni.

'He left in an illegal way and the landlord is begrudgingly looking for him to seek revenge,' they were told by a neighbour's wife.

'Revenge! What did he do?' asked Nandako, surprised.

'He broke into this house, they alleged, and made away with some items that had been seized due to unpaid rent arrears.'

'Wah, Lord, my son!' she exclaimed, not believing her ears.

'Are you his parents?'

'Yes, we are.'

'It's advisable for you to leave this place immediately because if the landlord gets to know of your presence, he may arrest you to pay for your son's damages and the rent arrears. I'm sure if anybody tells him that Situma's relatives are around, he will no doubt call the police!'

And so the parents had to leave the compound unceremoniously. Wanami, just like Nandako, was surprised at the strange turn of events but he concealed his frustrations by changing the topic of discussion now and then. Undeterred, they checked on Situma at Kentem Limited but still unknown to them, he had been fired long time ago. Desperate and dejected, with no one to tell them how to find Situma, the pastor and his wife boarded an evening bus and returned home.

A week later, Wanami received a letter which had delayed in the post office. The particular communication left the whole family devastated. The old man lacked words of comment. He left everything to God and attributed all the misery that his son was going through to the work of the devil.

'Lord save my family – my son in particular – from the bondage and yoke of satan; him the destroyer and You the builder,' he said in a monologue. He read the letter again.

Dear Dad,

Greetings! I hope you're fine. I'll be lying if I say I'm doing well here. Life is miserable and I'm sorry on what befell me and I fully bear the blame. I was sacked some days before I came home last year. I had intended to inform you about it but I became nervous and concealed the whole issue hoping to get another job soon.

At the moment, I'm leading a desperate life in the city. No job. No money. No food. I have sought employment everywhere but all in vain. Wherever I went, employers turned me away. Others gave me false promises that were never fulfilled. I've now resolved to do menial jobs available to earn a living.

I nowadays pull mkokoteni and at the end of the day, I get something meagre, for sustainance. I'm really sorry about this. I even moved from Marai Estate and I currently put up in Bondeni where houses are available at cheaper rates. Please I beg your forgiveness. Forgive me and treat me like your beloved son. I'm sure I won't let such a thing happen to me again.

Now I fully confess that what you told me is gospel truth: job seeking is harder than gold mining. I'm thinking of coming home but I don't have the fare. Once I get some money, I will come…and stay. Please bear with me. Thank you.

Your desperate son,

Situma.

*   *   *

Situma was standing beside his cart at the bus park waiting for customers. A middle-aged woman carrying a kid on her back and several luggage approached him. They agreed on terms of payment and soon Situma was loading his *mkokoteni*.

Wambete stood up from the bench where he was engaged in idle political chat with some city idlers and came to assist Situma. In the process of loading the luggage, he whispered to Situma the sinister motive he had in mind; lets rob this client.

The woman had two shiny briefcases, a sports bag and two carton boxes labelled 'handle with care'. The two cart-pullers suspected she was carrying something valuable. After negotiating the first corner in a corridor where there were no pedestrians, Wambete seized one of the briefcases and took to his heels. Situma dropped the cart and ran after him in pretence of pursuing a thief though he never raised an alarm.

Round the corner they went, nay, they ran, meandering through the maze of buildings and back street alleys. They were actually looking for a suitable hideout. The victim raised an alarm; she shouted thieves! This prompted a crowd of people to pursue the dual. The crowd was almost catching up with the suspected thieves when Wambete drew his pistol and pointed at them. Everybody fell down flat. The crowd retreated believing they had cheated death and regretted pursuing gangsters of Situma and Wambete's nature.

Within a short while, the police intercepted them. Situma's muscles weakened at the sight of a policeman pointing a gun at him. His nerves froze in fear and he fell on the ground, wishing that the earth could open and swallow him.

Wambete, a rude boy as he called himself, tried to escape but was shot on the arm. He fell down and rolled painfully in a pool of blood. People ran out of the buildings; shops, offices, and houses to witness the shooting drama.

The surging crowd bayed for the thieves' blood. They started pelting stones at the two hapless robbers but the police battled them with teargas canisters. Eventually, the commotion degenerated into a battle between members of the public and the police.

One of the police officers, in alleged self-defence, shot live bullets into the crowd, killed one person and injured several others. This upped the pandemonium characterised with total helter-skelter as people ran for their dear life with others now baying for the killer-cop's blood. In the fracas, scores of people were injured, property worth thousands destroyed and others of unknown value looted. Police later arrested several people in connection with the incident which they termed as 'obstructing police duty.'

Situma was taken to Kasembe police station in a Landrover whose windscreen had been shattered with stones. He stayed there for three days under torture. Wambete was hospitalised in handcuffs, his wound dressed, and discharged two days later to join Situma in a remand cell.

On the fourth day, the two jointly appeared before the chief magistrate's court where they were charged with robbery and illegal possession of a firearm. Their case was mentioned and set for hearing in a month's time. They were denied bail.

*   *   *

On the day of hearing, at 9.00 a.m., Situma and Wambete were taken through hurried court proceedings. They had nobody to defend them. Furthermore, no one from Namufweli attended the court proceedings. The family members were not aware that their son was undergoing a traumatising experience in the city.

Situma's eyes wandered all over the courtroom looking for a familiar face but there was none. Neither Nambozo nor Irene was present in court. There was a pin-drop silence as the judge passed the verdict. Guilty! Tears rolled down Situma's cheeks as a tall, stocky judge sentenced them to seven years imprisonment each with hard labour. Situma raised his hands and cried for mercy but he was whisked away by the officer who stood beside him in the dock.

The two were transferred to the main Karoko prison. Here, they were to be guests of the state for the next seven years. Situma was not so lonely in prison. He found Watima serving a two year jail term for stealing millions of shillings from Miami Financial Scheme. Inseparable indeed, as he had once told Nambozo.

'Situma, I have been sacrificed. That guy is not my uncle... I hate him. He used my signature to steal the money and promised to cover me if things went out of hand but he has now escaped leaving me in shit. He could have been here too but the court, for lack of evidence, set him free. I was found guilty… in fact let me say… I pleaded guilty. We planned it. I agreed to cover him up knowing that he would bail me out as well.

'He has the money… I banked it in his account… he advised me not to reveal anything, that he would withdraw the money and buy me freedom. But I was shocked last week when my mum came to see me, she told me the guy withdrew all the Sh. 10 million, believe it or not… it was ten M and has fled the country.'

*   *   *

Slowly, Situma started adjusting to prison life. He no longer shed tears of self-pity but rather opted to accept the reality and pray for quick passage of his jail term. Stories of freedom fighters who spend decades in prison and later came out to be presidents of countries inspired him.

'One day, I will leave this prison and vie for a leadership position in this country too,' he consoled himself. Regular visits by preachers and motivational speakers hardened him and encouraged him to take life as it comes.

Three months into their jail term, on the eve of Independence Day, several convicts were taken out to clear garbage along the main street that led to Karoko City Stadium where the Prime Minister was scheduled to lead the republic in the national celebrations. Among the convicts were Wambete, Situma, Watima and Marani, an inmate who had been imprisoned for murder-related charges that were later reduced to manslaughter after a successful appeal.

While collecting garbage near the African International Bank, a gang of robbers struck the bank and shot in the air several times, paralysing operations at the bank. Two prison wardens, who were guarding the inmates, sealed the bank premises to foil the robbery attempt and apparently forgot that they were guarding some other deadly thugs too. In the event, there was a fierce shoot-out between the wardens and the robbers.

Left unguarded, the four inmates escaped out of the city into Mareba forest.

Marani knew the particular hideout pretty well and was also familiar with the operations of thugs who often hid here when police hunted for them. In the hideout, they met with some other criminals who helped them throw away the prison attire and gave them new clothes, smart ones. They even shaved, showered and ate. In addition to this generosity, they also surrendered some guns to them. For defence against the law if it struck.

The following morning at 6.00 a.m., they resurfaced from their hideout with an intention of deserting Karoko City and never to come back again. Their destination was not specific, 'We shall just go wherever we feel safe provided it is away from the law,' they planned.

They had tested the bitter herbs in the city and did not wish to drink the water of affliction anymore. The urban lifestyle had taught them a lesson that none of them could wish to re-live. They quickly thought of getting a private vehicle that they could use to escape. Their prayer was to cross over to the neighbouring country, Weiza, if possible.

As they planned on how to go along with the heavy task ahead, they heard the sound of a vehicle coming from a distance. They thought it was a police car patrolling the area in their pursuit. So they took cover at strategic points where they monitored its approach.

'That could be a Landrover belonging to the boys, take care guys!' Marani warned.

'But wait…it sounds like a trooper,' observed Watima.

'Yah, the police can use any car to conceal their identity… We should be extremely alert and dangerous like spikes of thorns; and prick any one that shall attempt to fumble us. Even though they're armed, let's not be a walk over, they must trounce us after a thick sweat. We should survive by the gun or die by the gun,' said Marani.

'But as I was telling you last night, nowadays cops are easier people to trounce. They have the mentality that poorly-dressed people are imminent gangsters. They've never discovered that even a pick pocket dons a suit and a tie before he does his *fingering* business. We're so smart to be mistaken,' said Situma.

'Not exactly,' Wambete cut in, 'there was a time when they arrested a conman in one of the hotels last year dressed in a three–piece suit!'

'It seems his gods were not with him. All these things depend on luck sometimes, his star did not favour him that day making him to…' Situma did not finish his statement.

'Hey guys check the nice machine,' Marani and Watima said in unison.

As it came nearer, it turned out to be a Pajero with only a white woman behind the steering wheel. They stopped her and asked for a lift. She paid heed. They had not gone far when Watima, seated in front with her, drew a pistol and ordered her to stop. Frightened, she let her hands off the steering wheel prompting the Pajero to swerve sideways but Watima acted quickly and controlled it. He then behaved like a hangman who prays for the victim before tightening the noose. 'Next time, don't drive such a vehicle without the accompaniment of your husband, in case you have one,' said Watima.

They tied her hands and legs together; blindfolded her, robbed her of all the money and other valuables she possessed. They abandoned her by the roadside and sped off.

On reaching Bombori town, 100 miles from Karoko, the thieves took the stolen car to a garage where it was worked on beyond the owner's recognition. Originally it was dark blue but was now changed to red. The number plate was altered; it was given a foreign registration number similar to those used by diplomats. They knew such vehicles are hardly searched.

The Pajero was still under reconstruction when the four went to a nearby café for breakfast. Situma was gulping his tea when a newspaper vendor passed by. A screaming headline caught his eyes: CONVICTS ESCAPE. A sub-heading followed, 'Two suspects killed in a foiled bank robbery.' The whole story went thus: 'Two armed robbers were yesterday shot dead by Karoko Maximum Prison wardens and three others arrested when they attempted to rob the city's African International Bank branch. At the same time, four convicts escaped during the fracas and are suspected to have headed towards Mareba forest. A statement from the police headquarters yesterday said the officers are working round the clock to apprehend the escapees who are said to be very dangerous criminals…'

The passport size photos of Watima, Situma, Wambete and Marani were attached to the story and it was also reported that the Inspector General of Police had placed a reward of US $ 5,000 to anyone who would volunteer relevant information that could lead to the arrest of the convicts.

'Now, there is a heavy task ahead of us – battling with the cops,' Watima said after reading the newspaper and called his men to a private corner on the rear side of the garage where their vehicle was being worked on. 'We should be alert to avoid an abrupt ambush. The fat is now simmering in the fire. The news is all over… the cops are now trailing us, sniffing in every corner – vehicles, pubs, lodges, discos – to arrest us. Let's not linger here anymore; we better fly off before things boil up.'

He slipped the *new* Pajero on the highway and headed to Kinambi. Their plan still remained to go all the way across the border into Weiza. Their mode of dressing and the kind of vehicle they used concealed their identity as thieves and inmates on the run. They looked like diplomats. The Pajero, under the control of Watima, cruised at an average speed of 160 kph. The other three were on the look out to see if there was any suspicious vehicle trailing them.

At Ngamoi, a busy trading centre that was a favourite stop-over for truck drivers, the run-away criminals came into a huge police roadblock.

'Watima, even if they stop us, don't stop, let them pursue us or shoot. Don't show them white feathers or any sort of cowardice. We shall struggle to survive by the gun or die by the gun,' it was a command from Marani. He tapped his breast pocket to confirm if his pistol was still on him. They could see heavily armed policemen scrutinising vehicles with guns held ready. This was unusual especially in such a remote area. It made people sense that at least something was wrong somewhere.

When they approached the roadblock, one of the traffic policemen hurriedly removed the roadblock apparatus, saluted and waved them to proceed. Watima saluted back and pressed hard on the accelerator. After a short pause, he said to his colleagues as they sped off, 'that fool of a cop has just lost US $ 5,000 as it passes under his nose!' they all laughed, relieved, but did not celebrate crossing the hurdle yet, for they did not know what dangers lay ahead.

Kinambi was the next stop. The trio were not conversant with this rural town, so it was upon Situma, a Kinambi born, to lead the way. They had travelled all the way from Karoko, over 300 miles, but they did not feel the fatigue of such a long journey. Perhaps they could only feel tired after crossing the border into Weiza. It was 3.00 p.m. Situma took them to Walela, a businessman who owned a large automobile garage in town. He was willing to accord them accommodation but they declined the offer, fearing that any further delay could result to their capture.

Walela, forty-five, was a dark, tall man with a round face and a protruding tummy. His eyes, in spite of his age, were very alert and rarely blinked. He was a shrewd second hand motor-vehicle dealer who never wasted any opportunity to make money or acquire more wealth. It was alleged that he was formerly a thug, a specialist carjacker, but pulled out of active robbery when six of his gangmen were ambushed and killed by police after someone betrayed them. Rumour or no rumour, Walela's mode of operations could hardly pass the integrity test.

Kinambi town was suddenly full of police officers, both in uniform and plain clothes. Perhaps they had been tipped that the most wanted criminals were somewhere within the town. Information regarding heavy police and vehicles reached the four prison escapees through Walela's efficient coordination and spy network conducted by his accomplices. The four certainly had to escape. They changed the vehicle, left the Pajero with Walela and went with his Peugeot 504. They used rural rough roads to evade police dragnet. Walela escorted them until he made sure they had gone out of town safely. The border town was only thirty minutes' drive away. The prospect of operating from a foreign country made the four runaway convicts sigh with relief. This was the beginning of another chapter in their fugitive lifestyle.

*   *   *

At Kentem Limited, Nambozo was busy with office work in the morning when Musebe came in with a newspaper. 'Is this the bugger that used to work here? Check now, a most wanted criminal!' he said and threw the newspaper at Nambozo.

'I knew this boy was a potential criminal and I always suspected him of wrong doing. I never trusted him,' said Musebe.

'Oh my God… this is not true, no way no way, it's not true,' she cried after reading the first two lines.

Musebe looked at her in total disbelief. You sympathise with a criminal on the run? He threatened her with severe disciplinary measures but she was too emotional; she could not stop crying for Situma. Mad and angry, she took her handbag and stormed out of the office. She crossed over to the bus park and boarded a *matatu* home. She was filled with a mixture of feelings; angered by the media reports and worried about Situma's fate, especially if it was true that Situma had escaped from custody. This was her first time to learn that Situma had once been arrested, charged for robbery with violence, convicted and later escaped and now wanted by the police for the second time.

'Maybe it's another Situma Wanami, not my dearest Situma, I can't believe it… but this is exactly his face and his name.'

In her room, the five months old pregnant Nambozo got hold of the newspaper, looked at Situma's picture unbelievably, with tears rolling down her cheeks. She spoke to herself, loudly 'I love you Situma. For all this time I've been patiently waiting for you to come back from wherever you had gone and marry me… Situma, Situma, Situma please come back and prove to me that you're not the wanted fellow! I really need you here, my sweetie Situma!'

Her young cousin Cynthia, who entered the room unexpectedly, startled her.

'What's wrong Emma? Who are you talking to? Eeh…. your eyes are red and swollen, has someone beaten you?'

'Go away you silly brat!'

'But there is a…'

'I said go away! Leave me alone…' Nambozo was about to hit the young Cynthia but she dashed out and was only missed by a whisker.

Nambozo was so grumpy; a character she had never been known to possess before. Her aunt wondered why she had come home so early like this. She tried to speak to her but in vain. Nambozo just kept to herself in a thoughtful manner. Her aunt figured out that perhaps Musebe, the person she complained about frequently, had offended her.

'Is it Musebe… I mean, who did it?

'No, it's Situma,' she said solemnly and spoke no more.

The following day, while still preoccupied and disturbed by Situma's fate, Nambozo reported to the office and found a termination letter on her desk.

8

After crossing the border into Weiza, the quartet established a den in one of the towns, Kabemba. In the name of Economic Co-operation and Regional Integration, they passed off as potential investors.

In the new locale, they met a new acquaintance, Mukula, who was in his early thirties but with a disposition that suggested he was older. The seasoned gangster had bloodshot eyes that suggested either he rarely got enough sleep or was on drugs, or both. He was in charge of a gang of political dissents and members of a disbanded rebel militia unit now turned criminals. They had committed a host of heinous crimes, among them daylight robberies, cold-blood murders and rapes. He was in charge of a terror group for hire. They were often hired by dishonest politicians and wicked businessmen to kill potential competitors.

Mukula's group was a terror to the police network that occasionally became dumbfounded at the smartly organised operations. For years they evaded the long arm of the law by changing hide-outs at the slightest ripple in their calm abode. It was rumoured that they had informers among the police officers whom they paid protection fees. It was long before Situma and Watima began getting tuition and induction into the Mukula-led group's under-world operations. This was after a lengthy period of time during which someone proved allegiance and took oath of loyalty.

Marani and Wambete had all the delight in finding acquaintances that could come in handy to save them the situation of being vagabonds, for their short stay in Weiza had not opened any reliable avenues for livelihood.

This was a country where people were never in a hurry for anything. And if a new person came around and asked for a particular direction, one would just wish to take them there. People were very hospitable and humanity was given the first priority. Unlike their country where corruption and oppression of the common man were exercised loudly and proudly, where people had no courtesy and often shouted at each other, here life went on a bit smoothly with people having concern for each other.

After a three-month stay in Weiza under Mukula's pupilage and chaperon, Watima and Situma joined the gang for a mission to rob tourists visiting Kabemba National Reserve, situated in the remote parts of Eastern Weiza. The operation was dubbed *clean*: no violence, no killing, no leaving foot marks behind. They were to pose as game wardens escorting tourists.

'Watima,' Mukula the gang leader instructed him, 'you will be stationed near the park's gate but a bit far from where you can be noticed by the guards. Situma and I shall stay some distance away from the park and when they come, we shall stop them and possibly accompany them. As we get to you, Watima, I will introduce you as the security officer who will guide and guard them in the park.

'At that point, inform us that the main gate is under construction. We shall then diverge and use an alternative route. If they prove cooperative we shall take what we want and go away. And if they prove tricky, we shall skin them. Understood guys?' He spoke and suddenly paused, his eyes looking at everybody in the room.

'Nakalira, load the tool with enough lead… but avoid unnecessary violence… don't shoot to kill…. that should be our last resort.'

'What shall we do in case they're in the company of rightful tourist agents?' enquired Situma.

'They won't… it doesn't happen that way,' snapped Mukula. 'Those guys only accompany them while inside the park but not outside like we shall do. But in case things go unexpectedly, be on your best laurels – force and succeed by the gun or die by the gun. You'll be a hero.' But Situma was not convinced.

They spent the entire evening in a dark room behind the bar laying final strategies. Mukula and Watima dominated the speaking, an event that saw two crates of beer crushed down.

Occasionally, one of the game park officials, who happened to be in league with Mukula peeped in, had a word with him privately and left in a huff.

The criminal assignment ahead was the first one yet to be committed in a foreign country besides being unique in its own kind. It was the most risky one as Situma termed it. He even thought of pulling out though he feared the move could easily cost him his life.

'This criminal life made us desert our mother country. I feel we should not repeat the same mistake here. I prefer we look for some income generating activity to do and stop acts of robberies. We are professionals, we can still work here and earn an honest living, let's seek employment.' Situma implored Watima after they had parted with the other two. The latter advised Situma not to behave in a cowardly manner.

Watima could not figure out why his friend was not willing to take part in the mission. But having kissed the blarney stone, he succeeded in persuading Situma not to pull out of the forthcoming operation. This was accompanied by killer-threats such as 'You may not live to see the next day! Mukula will shoot you dead the minute you pull out of the gang!' Watima gave reassuring sentiments such as, 'We've taken the most risky and key roles, just register your presence with us and things shall go on well.'

The night before the operation was the worst ever for Situma. He did not sleep. Although he had been assured of success, he kept on worrying that the robbery may backfire and land them in hot soup. At night, he experienced insomnia as he kept debating with his inner self whether to participate in the crime or escape to a far away land from Mukula and company.

He finally, though half-heartedly, decided to be part of the robbery. In the morning he woke up with a lot of lassitude but because he had agreed to take part in the assignment, down to work they went. They arrived at the designated place on time and took their positions as earlier planned.

Watima was in the game warden's uniform, though he had covered it with a huge white apron. He took his place and the other three moved two miles away from the park. Mukula communicated with Watima regularly on mobile phone.

In a moment's time, at 10.00 a.m., the vehicle carrying the tourists came. It was a Nissan Combi, open on the roof. Mukula phoned Watima and advised him to throw away the white apron and be on the look-out. The trio then started walking towards the park direction so that it appeared they had a serious business ahead of them. Situma's heart throbbed fast. He stretched his hands and let out a lengthy yawn. Mukula whispered to him to pick courage and not to effeminate. Nakalira did not worry at all; he had his firearm intact. In case things went out of hands, he was ready to violently defend himself and the group. Occasionally, he tapped his breast pocket just to confirm if the weapon was still with him.

The Combi drew closer at a speed of about 20 kph, a speed that enabled the tourist to view and take photos of the beautiful scenery that surrounded the park. Excited tourists kept clicking their cameras as if they were in a competition. With a broad and courteous smile, Mukula flagged down the driver.

'Welcome to Kabemba National Park…,' he said.

'Thank you, we are grateful,' replied one of the lady tourists. They exchanged greetings and joked casually. Mukula introduced himself as a Tourist Guide Officer and proceeded to introduce his group to the tourists.

'This one,' he said pointing at Situma, 'is an Assistant Security Officer in the park,' Situma nodded appreciatively.

'The other one,' he pointed at Nakalira, 'is a Senior Government Official from the Ministry of Tourism, attached to this park.'

'Feel at home and enjoy yourself in our green country,' Nakalira chipped in.

Mukula reminded the tourists about the importance of their coming to Weiza and Kabemba in particular. He applauded them for their immense contribution to the growth of the tourism industry. The touring team was very delighted at Mukula's comments of appreciation and they greatly admired his good disposition. Little did they know that they were talking to rapacious wolves in sheep's skin.

Mukula told them that they were also heading to the park but their vehicle had broken down forcing them to trek this long. He asked the driver to offer them a hike for the remaining distance. It was granted without hesitation. Watima was alert wherever he was. When the white Nissan Combi approached with Mukula, Nakalira and Situma on board, he stopped and spoke to them with an apologetic tone. He had thrown away the white apron and was visible in full game officer's uniform. After identifying himself, with back up compliments from Mukula, Watima informed the tourists about the worst state of the route through the main gate and kindly requested them to use an alternative route that he volunteered to show them.

'Sorry for the inconvenience we have caused you. The main gate is not operational today. There is some infrastructural repairs underway. As an alternative, we are requesting our visitors to use the rear entrance.'

The tourists knew not that this was a group of masqueraders with ill motives. The soft speaking Watima, clad in game officer's uniform had sealed all the loopholes that could give them away. After all, who could suspect game officers robbing tourist? It had never happened in the country's history and the tourists held no slightest suspicion.

Watima misled them until they found themselves deep in the middle of a heavy forest. No house, no people, nothing. The gangsters who had propagated themselves as park officials and cicerones now acted, showing their true colours as robbers. The tourists were robbed of everything at gunpoint. They were tied on a tree and left to face own fate.

Situma did not actively participate in the crime; he brought up the rear when the three manhandled their victims. Consequently, Mukula cautioned him against such behaviour and urged him to be a man enough in the next assignment. He was, however, given his full share of the loot.

In the briefcases they found two digital cameras a pair of powerful binoculars and, to their surprise, a loaded pistol. Of great importance was the cash. Mukula, nobly and inoffensively, carried out the sharing process. He distributed a total of US $62,000 amongst the five people. Although the fifth member did not physically take part in the crime, all the success was attributed to him. Mukula kept the firearm. They parted ways as Watima and Situma moved further to Masera town.

The news about the robbery was soon out. It featured prominently in broadcast stations and newspapers. Foreign embassies were worried and prodded the government for quick action. The Minister for Security, flanked by his

Tourism counterpart, came out breathing fire and swore to bring the criminals to book. The police unit launched a manhunt for the culprits. Watima and Situma went into hiding; they kept indoors throughout and made sure not to interact with neighbours in their new abode.

Several days later the police spokesman announced what he termed as a breakthrough in the crackdown on robbers. He said five suspects had been arrested in connection with the park robbery. The statement further claimed that two of them had pleaded guilty of the crime while in police cells and were assisting the police with further investigations. Watima, Situma, Nakalira and Mukula were not among them. 'Then who are these people pleading guilty?' The four did not stop asking themselves. The guilty ones were to be arraigned in court soon, it was revealed further.

A month later Situma and Watima resurfaced as businessmen. They traded in electronic equipment. They made lots of profits and their names were entered into a list of local tycoons. With all the prestige, they resorted to luxurious lifestyle. Money was now not a problem and vaunting was the order of the day. They boasted of the immense wealth they had accumulated out of what they said was a result of their 'hard work.'

Ill got ill spent, so goes the saying. The two used to drink daily and excessively and at times they ended up sleeping in the bar. This happened to Watima one day and when he woke up at 5.00 a.m., he had been robbed over Sh. 15,000. Situma bought a vehicle and turned into a tourist of sorts. He was ever out visiting recreation places and taking his girlfriends for exclusive treats.

They say *a large purse commands a large crowd* and actually it did. An endless trail of women got attached to the two, and often fought for them. Unlike in their motherland where women love men because of love, here they loved because of wealth.

Life is indisputably circular; you go round and come back where you started. The two became broke again after squandering every cent, including their business capital. Their business outlet could not meet the variable costs and therefore wound up. They no longer showed off in pubs and suddenly their ladies deserted them. The state of paucity made them hide their faces from what they believed to be public mockery and humiliation.

9

◆ ◆ ◆ ◆

Marani, a short, stout man who always shaved his head clean walked the empty streets of Chili Town. He glanced at his expensive watch and with his piercing eyes surveyed the office blocks and the people walking up and down the streets. He knew Wambete could not miss to come on this particular hour to take on the assignment. Their mission was one that could turn them into overnight millionaires.

Occasionally, when he seemed convinced that Wambete would appear soon, his mind drifted yonder on how life would be sweet with the success of the day's plan. He could hear his girlfriend telling him:

You are my angel, oh my object of adoration,
Just swear by the moon and the stars
That you will marry none other than me
Promise Marani, just promise, nothing can stop you
From marrying me, just say a word.

In his wild dreams, he felt a friendly pat on his shoulder. He turned round smiling, 'Wambete, you're late for the...' but to his disappointment it was an old lady friend whom he had long erased from memory.

'Hi Marani,' she greeted him.

'Fine and still going strong,' he answered, detached from his words.

'Lost for long, where had you resorted to?'

'Nowhere actually... I've just been around... tied with a lot of business and other commitments.'

'And this morning you look busy still...let's go to my house for breakfast.'

'No let's arrange it for next time so that...' before he could pull in the words to the end, some rough disorderly footsteps that eventually graduated into tubs stopped just about the place they were to meet.

'Hi Marani, leave her alone, that's an after-work,' Wambete said and pulled him aside. Marani joined him in a hurry and thanked him for rescuing him from the whore. The lady was left wondering what they were up to. She looked at the two gentlemen walking down the street hurriedly but could still not tell what they were up to; even if she stood there for ages. All she could infer was that their deal involved some secret and that could have been the reason why Marani took off immediately Wambete appeared.

'Why do you include women in these deals?' asked Wambete as he lit a cigarette.

'I did not include her. I did not have any plans with her, leave alone giving her a hint of what's happening. We just met out there and she tried forcing herself on me.'

'Now, did you find out if Mwanika was joining us?'

'Yes, ah, see, there he comes, talk of the devil and the devil appears.'

'Hi Mwanika,' the two said in unison.

'Gentlemen, we're late and no more niceties. How far have you gone?' asked Mwanika.

'Many steps…we were just waiting for you, so let's go. Did you say the old man is left at home alone with the money?' asked Marani.

'Yes, all we have to do is threaten him… err… get hold of him, put a rope around his neck, point a gun at him and force him to produce the keys to the safe and automatically…we have all the money,' Mwanika put it so simply.

Keningo and Company used to pay its workers on the first Friday of every month. The proprietor's son had to go to the bank and withdraw the money a day before payments were made. Wambete, Marani and Mwanika had all these facts at hand. The company had over 1500 workers. The proprietor knew well that the security of the home was guaranteed, especially with the computer technology. He had surveillance cameras fitted around his compound and an automatic alarm linked to the police station. With such technology, he chose not to employ guards.

Mwanika was to break the alarm system, Wambete was to inspect the house and Marani was to do all the violence that goes with robbery. The trio had loaded pistols. Stealthily, they advanced towards Albhai's compound at 10.30 a.m. His son was not at home; the old man had been left alone with the money. The new house maid was also at home.

Albhai was making preparations to go and pay the workers in the afternoon. Marani, followed by Wambete rushed into the compound taking the route that Mwanika had taken. He noticed them and smiled scornfully when they pointed a gun at him. He was convinced that the security of the home was linked to the Central Police Station. The rich old man saw the thugs as people trying to do something totally impossible.

'*Mzee*, raise up your hands, co-operate and we shall spare you…' Albhai obeyed and led the thieves to the house. He knew it was a matter of time before the police arrived. They met Mwanika waiting for them at the stairs. The old man almost collapsed at the sight, but he reluctantly showed them the bedroom after they threatened to kill him.

Mwanika had made all the disconnections rendering the alarm system dysfunctional. Soon Marani got the first bag, second, third, fourth, fifth, oh sixth… 'We shall require a vehicle to carry all these,' he was surprised.

Helped by the old man, they collected all the bags containing the money and loaded them into an old Mercedes Benz parked in the compound. Mwanika took the driver's seat and soon they sped off.

Albhai was mercilessly pushed into the vehicle boot. It was locked and everything was going as planned; to have him dumped somewhere far where it would take quite a long time to reach the police or where it would take a hell of hours for his son to trace him. His bones made constant protest with *tik tik tok* as if they were breaking while being forced into the boot but the ruthless robbers did not care.

After a short distance, they stashed all the loot in one bag, abandoned the Mercedes by the roadside and broke into another vehicle. They drove further to Ketigoi village, over

50 kilometres away. Here, they parked the vehicle by the roadside and escaped on foot towards the forest.

The three robbers carried the money, meandered deep into the forest and after trekking for about an hour, they came to the end of the forest, crossed the village and settled in the compound of a local primary school. They counted the amount and to their amazement the mission had been overly successful.

Susan, the former maid who had given Mwanika all the information about Albhai and his household was to be given Sh. 50,000. They then shared the Sh. 2 million among themselves and parted ways.

'Take care, pals. See you as soon as a new mission comes by and beware of the government's sharp eyes and long arms; try to be rare…' said Mwanika as he parted ways with Wambete and Marani. He was very happy with over Sh. 600,000 stuffed in his pockets, with a pistol tucked in his hip pocket ready for self defence in case anything went wrong. His big jacket covered it. He now had his mind fixed on Susan who played a very crucial role in the operation.

At home, Susan believed her friend would come out successfully. She patiently waited like a vulture waiting to devour a carcass. The money she was to get would go to her family and domestic upkeep. *'Perhaps Gido, our neighbour, will respect and fear us too,'* she thought, *'she has always looked down on us. I will be a heroine. Yes, they will know that even a woman can generate money. How good and beautiful will I look? They will see me in a black jean and all the latest things… the best earrings… new handbag… oh…'*

She heard a slight knock on the door. Before she could open it, Mwanika dashed in and hugged her.

'Did it succeed?' she asked.

'Don't *papa*, be patient. I want something to eat first. I'm so hungry, my dear.' She gave him the food she had kept in her old cupboard for supper. With every swallow, a *gouud gouud* sound went down his throat. He swallowed enough so fast that he finished the plate of *ndengu* and chapatti in less than two minutes.

'Now I can speak... you know we just got hold of the guy and everything went on smoothly, unexpectedly and very successfully. Here is your share.' He handed her Sh. 50,000 in an envelope. 'I never knew that ladies of little importance like you could tear rich men into rags.' Susan, formally a house maid at Alhbai's household, was excited about the loot and she did not hear the ridiculous sentiments Mwanika was voicing out. Money. My money. Stolen money. She got perplexed.

Mwanika spent that night in her house. The following morning, he went to the local drapers and purchased a decent suit to disguise his appearance. He also bought himself a pair of spectacles and an umbrella hat.

In the evening, he felt disturbed but he could not figure out why. He went to Green Swallows Pub and took some beer just enough to scare off the anxiety that was building up in him. He did not intend to get drunk; he wanted to remain alert so as to catch any news doing rounds about the robbery.

Later in the day, it was announced over the radio that two ladies had been arrested in connection with robbery at Mr. Albhai and they were 'assisting the police with investigations.' One Hadija and another unnamed woman had been found drank in the backroom of a hotel and were abusing each other as they boasted of how much money they had, when the police seized them.

'Sure, could the other lady be Susan?' he asked himself. He began sweating. Saliva was sour on his tongue. 'What annoys me is that a deal with ladies gets leaked very easily.'

*   *   *

Watima was strolling lazily in the streets of Masera when he saw a heavily built man in a dark suit reading a newspaper in front of a hotel. He recognised him quickly. Wambete. He moved closer but before he could say a word Wambete also noticed him. They exchanged pleasantries and shortly, Marani appeared from the hotel. He too was smartly dressed in a jeans suit. Watima was happy to meet his friends who, to him, were almost fading off his memory.

'You are lost man, but I'm happy you're still alive and healthy too,' remarked Watima, as they sat in a secluded corner in a bar.

'And what have you been doing all this time, I mean… your source of income? What jobs did you get here?'

Wambete looked sideways to confirm nobody was around to grasp what he was about to whisper to Watima. Seeing nobody within earshot, he told them about the Albhai robbery and other subsequent operations they carried out.

'Did you hear of a supermarket that was looted three days ago? We were the men behind that mess. The boys must be hunting for us now…I'm sure,' he said, and handed a newspaper over to Watima which had reported that already five suspects have been nabbed in connection with the robbery and are to be charged in a court of law soon!'

'I tell you the police in this country are just like ours at home. They are fond of arresting wrong fellows. But sometimes the trap meant for a rat can bind a kitten, anyway.'

Watima too informed them about the operation at Kabemba National Park that saw them become instant millionaires. He also talked about other small-scale robberies that followed later.

The four 'brothers', after being re-united, moved farther to another part of Weiza, Butanga, where they established a den. Situma was happy to meet his lost comrades whom they had suffered the same fate and drank from the same pot in Karoko. They endlessly reviewed their past lives in Karoko, with a mixture of hate, regrets and passion.

I miss home, contemplated Situma. Once I get money, I will dodge these guys and cross back home … yes, home to mum and dad, sisters and brothers. I will definitely go back…eh…sneak back home. Yes, and find Nambozo… oh… Irene.

Life without money became truly unbearable. Occasionally, a day could end without tasting a meal. Paying bills like rent, water and electricity turned tricky. The brothers-in-crime put their heads together in an attempt to forge a way of survival. They unanimously agreed to go for an operation to earn a living. They had committed a host of crimes and got so much money but the urge to rob kept recurring.

So this evening they planned to rob a wholesale in Butanga town. Wambete and Watima had pistols so they laid a strategy on how to storm the premises. Watima proposed the attack strategy. 'Once we get in, the normal procedure will be followed. I will shoot in the air to scare customers, if there will be any. Wambete, swiftly, nay, let me put it like this, immediately after the gun shot, you'll jump across the counter and grab the cash… don't care about other things… just cash. Don't even mind about your security; you'll be under protection from us…'

They sealed the suspicion loopholes through designing suitable attire for the operation. They managed to acquire a blue Peugeot 504 for the job. Situma named this robbery a 'once-and-for-all' case for he never intended to take part in any other form of theft, whatsoever.

He had plans of crossing back home after this nefarious venture and hide deep in Namufweli village. He planned that the proceeds from the operation would be used as transport back home. He needed a break from this hectic world and the entire kind of lifestyle that he had found himself in. He still strongly thought of Nambozo and Irene, 'If I find any of them still waiting for me, I will marry and settle down.'

In the morning they set ready for the job, all of them nicely clad in suits and ties. At 9.30 a.m., after crushing down a bottle of whisky to boost their morale, they parked their vehicle outside the wholesale. Watima stepped out and felt his breast pocket to confirm that his pistol was with him. Yes, it was intact. The pistol that Situma carried did not have a single bullet; it was only meant for scaring purposes. All the key roles had been left to Watima; covering the cashier, patronising Wambete and making sure that no one could cause a ripple, however slight. He was known to be a sharp shooter; an intrepid attacker, with perfect degree of celerity.

He gave an eye signal and Wambete, who carried a small briefcase, reciprocated through the same medium. Situma smiled at Marani. This time, he had high hopes of success and was certain that after the robbery, he would cross back to Namufweli, purchase a piece of land, look for Nambozo or Irene, whoever could come first, and marry.

The trio entered quietly into the wholesale and posed as customers.

'Which of the two brands do you think we should purchase?' Wambete pretended to consult with Situma loud enough to be heard by the salesman behind the counter.

'We'd rather take the English brand, many buyers like it... it sells faster,' Situma suggested.

Watima moved closer to the man at the counter and pretended to be inquiring something from him but in the event he drew a pistol and ordered the now frightened man to surrender. On seeing the ugly muzzle of a pistol pointed at him, he quickly raised his hands in total submission and pleaded with the robbers to spare his life. Wambete acted swiftly. He located the cash box and emptied all the money in the bag. Situma patronised him as Watima took care of the harmless cashier.

Hardly had they made away with the loot than they heard a deafening gun shot. It penetrated through Wambete's back ripping his chest. He died instantly. The briefcase in which he had stashed the cash fell on the floor and scattered its contents. Watima was caught unawares. He attempted to run out of the premises in a bid to escape but it was too late; a bullet hit him on the head. He fell down on the floor at the entrance, not far from Wambete. Dead.

With their mission nipped in the bud, Situma ran out of the wholesale in a bid to enter the vehicle and escape, only to find that Marani had driven off. Situma now had to run for his dear life. The armed security officer who had been deployed to guard the wholesale from a vantage point above the ceiling, shouted at Situma to stop, but the latter instead picked speed. The guard pursued him. Situma took him round the nearby forest in what would be a tough marathon race.

The guard had shackles intending to arrest Situma and possibly hand him over to the police. He managed to catch up with Situma but could not single-handedly handcuff him. Eventually a physical fight ensued; Situma gave him two electrical blows on the head that sent him staggering to the ground. Proving hard to beat, the security man gained balance quickly and charged at Situma furiously. He applied tae-kwon-do style of kicks, but Situma dodged and his combatant hit the air hard and fell with a heavy thud on the opposite side. He attempted to compose himself, gain balance and stand up, but too late, Situma was already on top of him. He gave him heavy blows on the face and kicks on his chest and sent him rolling back to the ground and whining painfully – a sign of defeat.

Situma, charged with fury, picked a piece of wood lying nearby and hit the assailant on the head. The guard showed signs of dying soon and that is exactly what Situma intended. He wanted to kill him to avenge for the deaths of his fallen accomplices. He quickly grabbed the guard's pistol, aimed at him and pressed the trigger, only to discover that it was bulletless. The two bullets he was assigned had already been spent on Watima and Wambete.

He then sat on the security man's back, who now lied face down, and continuously banged the back of his head with the barrel of the pistol as if he wanted to open up the skull and see what lay inside. By now the man on the ground was groaning painfully - half dead - and could not fight back.

Convinced that his mission was complete, Situma was on the verge of taking off when the police arrived at the scene immediately. He could not stand to be arrested. He attempted to run for his dear life but was shot on the leg and immobilised.

The dire consequences of his nefarious acts were now being meted on him in large quantities. He wished the earth could open up and swallow him. He, apparently, envied Watima and Wambete who were already dead and were nowhere to go through the bitter experience he was undergoing. He cursed Marani and accused him of failing them. 'I will just kill him, if we ever met.'

Outside the wholesale, a crowd of curious on-lookers milled around watching with horror as the two bodies lay in a pool of blood and the scattered money on the floor. Police came to the scene and took the bodies away.

Situma was arrested and taken to Butanga Police Station under tight security although it was obvious that he could not manage to escape owing to his broken leg. On interrogation, it was discovered that he was a foreigner in that country. Police made an emergency call to Karoko Central Police Station to report the matter and it was quickly agreed that he be extradited to face criminal charges in his mother country, including robbery with violence and escaping from lawful custody.

Situma was immediately flown back to Karoko in a police chopper and handed over to the authorities where he was a most wanted criminal, having escaped from lawful custody.

*　　*　　*

Rumours travel faster than wild fire. The grapevine news already had it that Situma died on that fateful morning of the robbery. When this information reached Namufweli village, the parents were distraught with bitterness. They mourned Situma.

Nandako rent the air with a spine-chilling scream that summoned the neighbourhood. Soon everyone in the village was aware of Situma's death. Villagers conversed in low tones wondering what the cause of death could have been. Wanami consulted with other elders on what was proper following the death of their son hundreds of miles away from home. This was after futile attempts had been made to trace the body. Moving from morgue to morgue bore no fruits either.

Customarily, a mock burial was to be performed to be followed by a cleansing ceremony to appease the spirits; for it was believed that whoever dies in the bush may return to torment the living. Thus, Situma was to be accorded a decent burial. A full and proper burial ceremony was to be carried out, with or without the body; it was agreed amongst elders, despite resistance from a section of religious leaders.

Wanami, distressed by the death of his son whom he considered the saviour of his family, one who could have unshackled him from the yoke of poverty, went through the whole process absent mindedly. He tried to behave as if all was well, but his body language betrayed his emotions.

The case of Situma's missing body however took a new twist when it was announced over the radio that an unidentified body of a thug shot dead by the police along the border about a fortnight ago was still lying at the mortuary. It was said to belong to a middle-aged man though its eyes had been gorged out and the head disfigured by gunshot. According to the descriptions, the height was similar to Situma's 5'8. The body size was like Situma's and more confusing, the jacket that the dead man wore was exactly the type that Situma used to have. Parents, friends and relatives who had gone to view the body unanimously agreed that this was Situma's body. After settling the matter with the police and mortuary authorities, they took the body home for burial.

'God created man from dust… and unto dust shall man go… God giveth life and God taketh life….' said the Reverend during the funeral mass. He told the mourners that 'these were the last days of our lives' and advised them to whole-heartedly devote themselves to God and not to treat Him like a vehicle's spare wheel that is only opted for whenever a puncture occurs.

Life is only but a privilege
Death is a must
But no one knows the time
When, how and where
Death shall strike.
It creeps slowly
And stealthily and wickedly
Like a thief at night
Who cannot be predicted
Stay awake, dear mortal
And keep vigil the whole night
For a thief shall come any moment

Emotions ran high and tears flowed freely as the 'body of Situma' was lowered into the grave 'to rest in eternal peace.' Nekoye was there to mourn her husband-to-be. *'Maybe God never intended it, but I liked him; I loved him.'*

The impact of what happened gripped Wanami a few days later. He became so heart-broken and even questioned the religious conviction and concepts that guided him. He accused God of throwing him into Satan's trap. 'Oh God, dear Lord, the saviour of mankind, You have deserted me at an hour when I needed You most. I have served You faithfully, but sinners seem to prosper more…' the visibly depressed old man muttered.

Nonetheless, he had to come to terms with realities of life after mourning for days. He tried to forget the death of his son but with little success; it kept recurring in his mind. He thought of Situma deeply and suspiciously. Who killed my son? What did he do to deserve such a cruel death? Why should people kill each other? Who decreed that?

Nandako seemed to have adjusted faster and she constantly reminded her husband to thank God, for He gives and takes away life, and that God does everything in this world with a purpose. She tried to bring him to understand that human beings are mortals and they shall not live forever. But as much as Wanami tried to adjust and face the reality, he sometimes stared blankly into space and nodded in disapproval.

One day, he revealed a dream that had constantly nagged him to a group of his age mates.

'This always happens after such an experience… It shouldn't bother you. Remember the time I lost my wife; I had such dreams for over a year. Take heart, it will soon be over,' an old man remarked.

Wanami did not hear that. No words could convince him otherwise. His dream, as he called it, was real. The vividness of the dream could not be taken for granted, he insisted.

'The latest dream I had was yesterday,' he paused. 'After my evening meal, I went to bed. I caught a light sleep. My son shyly came to me and his battered look shocked me. He said 'father it wasn't my wish to desert you. I wouldn't do that… I have suffered enough and I beg your pardon.' Before I could respond, he walked away. I turned in bed wondering.'

He nodded again in disapproval and summarily told fellow old men that he strongly believed his son was still alive somewhere. Half of the old men dismissed him as an anguished *mzee* at the sudden loss of his son. The party later broke with others suggesting a proper cleansing ceremony.

For several weeks, the same dream kept recurring with the same vividness and almost the same message, something that astonished Wanami. The church, as a matter of intervention and doctrine, came to Situma's graveyard, laid a wreath and offered special commemorative prayers to drive off the 'evil spirits' that regularly tormented Wanami. The *balokole* fraternity strongly believed this was an evil spirit in pursuit of the children of God.

*   *   *

After the Weiza government extradited him back to Karoko, Situma was handed a thirteen year jail sentence after pleading guilty to a host of crimes including robbery with violence, illegal possession of firearms, and worst of all, escaping from lawful custody. This time, he was put under solitary confinement and was never allowed to see the sun at any one moment.

A month later, he was transferred to an island prison over 50 kilometres off the coastal town where he could not be reached and could not risk escaping either. Here he joined dozens of political prisoners jailed for opposing the ruling regime. Most of them were serving life imprisonment for treason related charges.

Demonstrations against the regime of the day were a frequent occurrence in Karoko City and other towns across the country. People often marched in streets demonstrating against the mysterious deaths of politicians. They were fed up with all manner of impunity, political assassinations and dictatorial tendencies of the Prime Minister who had ruled the country for more than 20 years. They yearned for political change.

Although the country got independence long time ago, the people here looked forward to what they termed as 'second liberation.' The economy of the country had deteriorated and was down on its knees thanks to large-scale corruption and theft from the public coffers orchestrated by senior government officials. Corruption was exercised in public places openly and public jobs were only given to deserving tribes and the politically correct individuals.

In order to continue ruling, the Prime Minister had orchestrated ethnic clashes to split the masses along tribal lines in order to achieve his wicked aspirations of divide and rule. He made communities to regard their neighbours as enemies. Opposition leaders attempted to unite the masses but the government was quick to curtail their efforts. Whenever opposition leaders held public meetings, police were quick to disperse them violently. The government had turned to be a burden to the development of the people, posing as a stumbling block in almost all ventures of development. Instead of serving the people, it sucked the national resources and impoverished them. The Prime Minister believed that poor people were easier to rule.

An opposition leaders' meeting had once been organised at a city stadium but police warned people not to attend, terming it illegal. The organisers defied the orders and went ahead to convene the meeting. Defiant citizens attended in large numbers, estimated at over 200,000.

'We are living in an era of oppression… the current government is composed of murderers and thieves who have reduced the dignity of our citizens to refugees and slaves… We have been made slaves in our own country! But I can see light at the end of the tunnel. My government will be a government of the people and the nation will be empowered both politically and economically…' the crowd yelled as the chief opposition leader, who was tipped to ascend the presidency in the forthcoming general election, spoke. 'The current government can best be described as a tired one. And the best favour we can give it is to vote it out of power… they have lost the sense of direction and the Prime Minister himself is now politically bankrupt…,' he said as people flashed their political party salute, chanting, 'He must go! He must go! He must go!'

Before long, hundreds of policemen cordoned the stadium and lobbed tears gas canisters at the crowd. A stampede ensued as people engaged the police in running battles that spilled to the city streets. Over 10 people were shot dead while hundreds got injured in the melee. The opposition leader was arrested and charged for alleged incitement of the masses to violence.

*   *   *

It was the second year of Situma's jail term at the island prison when the chief opposition leader won the country's elections with a landslide victory. People sighed with relief and hoped that sanity would finally be restored in the country. They hoped for a better nation and better living standards. The new Prime Minister immediately announced a reprieve for all political prisoners specifically those that had been jailed in the island prison. Situma's name was inadvertently listed amongst this group and he too was set free.

*   *   *

The afternoon showers had resulted in a chilly weather. Situma looked out of the bus window and saw heavy mist covering the hilltops as sunset drew closer. In the bus, excited citizens talked about the new government and how it was inclined towards fighting corruption. Parcels of public land that had been grabbed or illegally allocated were being recovered. Under the new regime, traffic police were now disciplined. Unlike in the past when they openly received bribes and allowed offenders to get away with serious traffic offences, this time the bus carried its capacity and there was no money changing hands between the police and the bus conductors.

They reached Kinambi town at 7.00 p.m. Still he had about 10 kilometres to go. Furthermore, he seemed a stranger in his hometown. Of all the things, he had forgotten the route to Namufweli village. He boarded a wrong *matatu* heading back to Ngamoi only to be re-directed by a woman who sat next to him.

7.30 p.m. The town was deserted and there were no signs of vehicles coming to pick passengers since all the public service vehicles had closed for the day and taxis could not be spotted around either. Some commuters abandoned their journey and sought accommodation in town but Situma had the determination to reach home and meet his family members, even if it meant walking on foot deep into the night. He was left alone at the bus park optimistically waiting for public means to take him home. He had a rare determination to meet his people after such a long separation.

After a short while, he spotted a white car in a nearby petrol station. He thought it was a *matatu*.

'Hallo, which route are you plying?' Situma asked.

'Which route! To where?' the driver sounded rude.

'I mean, is this not a *matatu?*'

'No. It is private… and I'm going somewhere deep in Namufweli.'

'I'm also going there please…' Situma got relieved and excited, 'but it appears impossible to get any means at this hour, don't leave me behind please, for kindness sake,' Situma begged him.

'Are you a visitor in this town? Vehicles here don't operate at night,' said the driver who finally agreed to offer him a lift. On the way home he asked Situma, 'where, in particular, are you going? Whose home?'

'Pastor Wanami's home…'

'Oh, the Pastor, are you his son?'

'Yah, of course, I am'

'I see…um… sorry for what befell you. I heard that your elder brother called Situma who used to work far away in Karoko City passed away… I had never met him myself… I only used to hear about him.'

'That's how the world is, people come and go,' said Situma.

Though he was totally dumbfounded at the revelation, he stayed calm and took things the way they came. At least, after his long absence, he expected to hear such type of news. Although he was surprised at his apparent death, he could not openly show his consternation to the driver. He concealed the grim feelings and feigned composure but he could still not hide everything; he looked disturbed and deep in thoughts. The driver concentrated on the steering; he never looked sideways to steal glances at Situma. This was a rough road and he had to exercise maximum concentration lest he hit into potholes.

'Situma died? What killed him? So I'm dead and buried! This is unbelievable!' They reached the junction where the driver was to diverge and proceed to his employer's home. He brought the engine to a halt and, for the first time, took a glance at Situma. He realised that the man he carried was so weak, weary and tired. He pitied him.

'You seem unwell…I mean, you look quite sickly,' the driver pitied him.

'Yes, I've been very sick lately. In fact, I went to town this morning for treatment… I have a chest problem and whenever it worsens, it makes breathing difficult for me. And fever has never deserted me for the last one week,' Situma lamented.

'Ay, *wase*, sorry, I wish you a quick recovery.'

As Situma opened the passenger's door to alight, the driver stopped him, 'Please wait. You can't walk that long distance in such a poor state of health. Let me drop you a bit nearer. You know the owner of this vehicle,' he said as he engaged the gear, 'is one of the harshest and meanest people I've ever come across but I hear he grabbed a plot in Kinambi town and the new government is now on his neck... They will tear him into pieces, I like that...' he said, laughing. Situma did not join the debate.

The family members were seated in their father's new house; the house he built using the money he was given as consolation after the death of his son. They were conversing and cracking jokes before retiring to bed when they heard a slight tap on the door. Everyone wondered who it was, calling on them so late in the night. Due to many crime incidents in the area, they dared not open the door until the caller identified himself.

'Who's knocking?' Nandako asked.

'It's me...' Situma said with a husky voice.

'You? Who? What's your name,' she insisted to know the person behind the door. Still there was no response. Situma just ignored her and continued knocking hard on the door.

Wanami stood up and unlocked the door. His family members were stunned at the appearance of Situma who they had buried two years ago. They were all horrified and were sure this was an evil spirit that had come into their home to torment them. His brothers and sisters including Nandako ran out. Waliaula was not around by the time.

Wanami called them back asking them to remain calm but in spite his assurance, everyone looked frightened. Catherine could not imagine mixing freely with a supposed ghost, and so did Fred and Gladys.

'Father... father, I am not dead. I am alive but I have suffered a great deal out there. The world has been so hostile to me. It captured me and tortured me mercilessly...but father I'm back. I'm happy to be with you again...' Situma cried and hugged his father.

Nandako came back, cried and hugged her son. 'Are you really the one? I can't believe it.'

Situma had changed completely. He appeared shaggy, emaciated and even aged. He was no longer the handsome, energetic, spick and span young man that people used to know. He had a lot of scars on the face and head which he received as part of 'discipline' given by the police to the inmates. He was limping as well.

The news about what was called the *resurrection* of Situma reached all corners of the village very early the following morning. By 8.00 a.m., everyone was aware of the extra-ordinary event that had occurred the previous night. People received the news with mixed feelings. Some were happy about Situma's comeback and they rejoiced. Others took it as a bad omen; a sign that something fatal was bound to happen. They cautioned villagers against such mysterious occurrences. Curious men, women and children alike flocked the pastor's home to witness 'the resurrection of Situma.' Some only came to confirm if the rumour was true. Many could not believe that Situma, for all that time, was alive somewhere and had finally returned home.

Wanami gave a reported account of his son's tribulations telling them how he had been languishing in prison and how he had it rough with the Weiza authorities where, it was claimed, he had gone to seek employment. But the doubting Thomases maintained that the real Situma died and was buried; and his ghosts had just visited the village and possibly will go back with some lives.

The elders could not figure out when such a thing happened last in history. Most of the villagers stayed at the fence. They were too frightened to enter into Wanami's compound despite their curiosity to see and know more about this strange happening. Just like a plaque, they avoided any form of contact with Situma.

'Exactly, you see, that's not a human being. It's a ghost, I told you, look at the head, too big for a normal human being, and the legs, so thin... look at the hands, just like sticks, and the body is more of bones than flesh... eeh that's how a ghost looks like. Beware people. Wait. You'll see and hear what's going to happen soon,' some people were heard speaking across the fence when they saw Situma.

*   *   *

The ceremony to exhume the body that was mistakably buried in Wanami's compound was duly performed. The body was handed back to the authorities, the graveyard cleansed and everything seemed to be forgotten at once. But this left the family with a big question mark. Was this real or imagined? Will things, with time, turn round again?

Everybody wondered. Wanami regretted relying on rumours to carry out such a grave function that in the long run left him with eggs on the face. All in all, he prayed for the passage of time to clear the memory and heal the wounds.

10

A year had passed since Situma *resurrected* and everybody was finally convinced that Situma did not actually die. He stayed at home nursing the prison hangover while trying to retrace his good old life again. The new government had promised to create at least 500,000 jobs annually and Situma was optimistic that one day, he would secure a job with the government.

Waliaula had graduated from the TTC and was now teaching at Namufweli Primary School. The government provided free primary education and many children had turned up for the offer, with many teachers being employed. The talk about increasing teachers' salaries was also doing rounds.

Bored in the village, Situma thought of going back to Karoko to seek employment but this did not go down well with his father. It prompted Wanami to talk bitterly about Situma's past record in the city, which he termed 'wanting and shameful.' Situma felt offended. He got annoyed and decided to leave home without his father's consent to seek employment in town and stay away from what he termed as 'frustrations of the old man.' The following morning, he left home early leaving behind a note addressed to his father.

Dear Dad, I seem to be a black sheep in your good family and so I've decided to pave way for you. Anyway, I'm gone but don't worry much about my whereabouts. Only believe that I'm safe somewhere within the universe. Pass my greetings to Mum, Catherine and our dear little Fred, I'll miss their company very much. Otherwise worry less about my departure.

Situma.

On arrival at Manga town, 100 miles away from home, Situma was tired and hungry but he had no money to buy a meal. He sat on a bench outside a drapers shop and borrowed a newspaper from one of the vendors to keep himself busy. He nostalgically remembered the good old days in the city.

Time flew fast. It was 2.00 p.m., within a short time 4.00 p.m.; and in another short while darkness had crept in. The first and major problem was accommodation. He knew nobody in town and had no money to book a hotel either. That night, he slept on the cold pavements in the company of street urchins who attempted to force him to sniff glue but he fought them off.

The following morning, he caught a severe malarial fever accompanied with running nose. He visited Manga District Hospital for treatment. Patients were so many and he queued over 20 metres away from the Doctor's Examination Room. This being a government hospital, no levy was imposed on patients thanks to the new government policy of free medicare. He was examined and given anti-malarial drugs at the outpatient wing. On his way back from the hospital, he wondered where to go next.

The midday sun was hot. He entered a nearby restaurant to drink some water. Luckily, at the restaurant he met his former schoolmate Muranda, who was working as a Sales Executive with Mamba International Ltd.

'Eer… Do you work here in town? Congratulations *bwana*. It's been long. I even thought you died many years ago,' joked Muranda as he hugged his long lost pal. His joke was a bitter one. Apparently, he was making fun about something that had truly happened; something that Situma did not wish to hear at all.

'How are you pushing on with life?' enquired Muranda.

'Not bad. I'm just on my way trying to pursue my luck wherever it's hidden.'

'But I thought you were working somewhere. The last time I met Waliaula in Kinambi he told me that you were with Kent something Company in Karoko.'

'Yah… its called Kentem Limited. I was there briefly under a certain brute who made life so difficult for me until I pulled out. I'm now hanging and floating. I've been moving up and down trying out different places but with little success. In fact, I'm ready to work as anybody, even as a house boy, as long as I get paid,' he said.

'You are not serious, Situma,' said Muranda. 'You are well educated; you can't work as a domestic servant.'

'But lately, even graduates roast green maize by the roadside or set up small *kiosks* and *kinyozi* to earn a living. White collar jobs are truly scarce but I'm hopeful of securing government employment. Recently we attained independence, we voted snakes and ghosts out of government and I believe the new system is going to be mindful of people's welfare. They will give us jobs.'

Situma disclosed all his problems to Muranda who helped to solve the few he could, including immediate ones like offering accommodation and little pocket money to facilitate job seeking. He put up with Muranda as he tried out different places.

At last he was employed with a publishing firm as a magazine vendor, a casual position in respect to his academic qualifications. The publishers housed him in a small single room, the same size as that of Bondeni which served as a kitchen, bedroom, living room, and store; just everything. Work here was cumbersome, toiling the whole day with magazines in the streets, only to sell a few copies by the end of the day. The number of copies sold determined the salary. Few sales meant little commission and vice-versa.

'*Society… Society* Magazine for the latest news updates, styles of attire and all the leisure…' Situma shouted in the street to attract potential readers. 'Sister come closer and get yourself a copy and know more about lifestyle…' Situma spoke to a lady customer. She moved closer and perused through the magazines; she liked them and bought herself a copy. Situma looked at her and acknowledged her beauty; he admired her.

'Hi sister, you look familiar… where did we meet?'

'You've seen me here today of course! Where else?'

'But it looks like…' before he could finish his statement the lady walked away. 'Hey, please come back,' he said but she proceeded on in a huff. After all, women are like *matatus*… you miss one and wait for another. She is not the only fish in the pond, the naughty Situma consoled himself.

A week later, the same lady passed by again and scanned the papers. Situma took caution not to say anything careless lest he stirred the hornet's nest.

'How are you doing?' she greeted him.

'I'm doing wonderful,' he said. She smiled and asked how wonderful he was.

'In providing the best information to the public at a cheaper price… through the vibrant *Society* Magazine,' said Situma. She bought a copy and went away smiling at the comedian Situma.

The little commission that Situma earned out of selling magazines was all squandered in the bar. He drank more and ate little, dealing a big blow to his health. He had a lot of domestic problems but whenever he got money he 'forgot' about them only to regret after squandering every cent. He never thought of helping his parents this time round. He did not even call home. Either he was annoyed with people at home or was simply not interested.

One day he was relaxing in his house reading a copy the *Society* Magazine. He was off duty. The article on why ladies lie about their ages interested him most. The writer had argued that ladies prefer to be 'younger' so that they remain 'marketable.' He later took a stroll downtown. Passing through the streets, he entered the main bookshop just to look at some of the novels they stocked.

While moving through rows of books he bumped into this lady who had become his regular customer. She was holding Sidney Sheldon's book: *Stranger in the Mirror*. They exchanged greetings and she asked Situma if he was still wonderful. 'Of course I still remain the wonderful one,' he said. 'My name is Situma Wanami,' he took the opportunity to introduce himself rather formally and cautiously. He was not sure if she was interested in knowing him and if she was willing to let him know her either.

'Pleasure meeting you Situma, I'm called Natasha Buluma,' she said and gave him her business card. She worked as an administrative officer with an advertising and public relations agency.

'Have you read this book?' Situma asked pointing at Sheldon's novel that she was holding.

'Not yet.'

'It's a very wonderful piece,' he said, ' I read it almost five times and I really enjoyed that character Tobby Temple so much.'

'Which other novels do you have?' she asked him.

Situma mentioned John Grisham's *The Partner* and *The Chamber*, Cynthia Freeman's *The Days of Winter*, Jeffrey Archer's *Kane and Abel, In the Name of the Father*, among others.

'How will I get them, please?' she asked. He promised to bring her some books the following day at his place of work. When they met the next day, Situma was at his usual *Jua kali* stand selling magazines and newspapers. She greeted him with a simple 'hi' and he answered with all the courtesy of a gentleman, 'I'm very fine, madam.' They chatted casually, still trying to know each other, and Situma gave her a free copy of the *Society* Magazine. He had also brought her two novels as promised.

In the course of their interaction, they started opening up to each other. Situma told her how good he usually felt when the two were together and how dejected he became when they parted. He admitted having fallen in love with her. She did not comment.

After weeks of what was considered 'general friendship,' that was characterised with evening coffee meetings, Situma invited her to his house so that she could know where he stayed. He knew that she lived in a mansion in a high class estate but he did not fear inviting her in the *ghetto*, as he used to call his low-class residence, so that she could see his humble abode. She declined to visit him, citing lack of time due to work commitments but Situma insisted that she just spares a few minutes 'to pass by.' They fixed the date for a Sunday evening.

On the eve of their meeting, Situma visited Muranda and asked him for a soft loan.

'There's a lady coming to see me but I don't have any cent to give her a treat. I'm miserably broke *bwana*. Please get me some chums, I will refund you later.'

'Which lady? From where?'

'Eer... she is called Natasha just from Manga town. She works with Jupiter Limited.'

'Natasha Buluma?' he asked, detached.

'Exactly, that is her name, a tall brown figure.'

Muranda bit his lips with resentment and bitterness. He looked at Situma with an evil eye. He too had been seeking Natasha's hand in love but with no success. He sent her several passionate messages but she never responded. She always received his messages, read them, threw them aside and laughed.

The previous Christmas, he sent her a card and a bouquet of flowers and invited her for dinner but she never turned up. 'I don't like this guy, he is boring,' she once told her friend. And whenever she met Muranda in town, she greeted him casually, excused herself and quickly moved on. But the man was quite optimistic, he believed that one day she will calm down and they would talk about love. He chose to give her time to soar high into the sky before she eventually came down to earth.

Now, to learn that the lady he was patiently waiting for had easily agreed to date another man – moreover a man of no means – was a very tasteless revelation. He boiled with fury and thought of punching Situma but he controlled his emotions. He apparently felt that Situma was interfering with his plans of marrying Natasha. Muranda sighed heavily and shook his head in disbelief.

'I tell you I'm very broke... I don't have money to lend you today,' he said. Then there was prolonged silence. After some interval Situma attempted to break the silence,' Have you read this week's copy of *Society* Magazine? It has a portrait of the world footballer of the year...' but Muranda was not listening.

He erupted into a rage and spewed out what was burning inside him. 'How did you come to know that girl, Situma?' he asked. Before Situma could answer, Muranda went ahead to accuse him of an attempted upstage.

'But how?' Situma protested.' I'm not aware that you two are in any relationship. I'm not aware that you have an affair with her. I have never seen you with her! But if that's the case, I'm sorry and I'll never speak to her again. I will pave way for you my friend… please carry on with her…' Situma said though he knew deep inside him that keeping off Natasha for Muranda's sake was nonsense. If anything, he was simply inviting Muranda to join him in a neck-throttling competition for her. That evening they parted on a very sour note.

On Sunday evening, Natasha turned up at Situma's house as agreed. The weather was chilly prompting her to wear a black jeans trouser and a heavy jacket. She sat on Situma's bed – there was no furniture – and praised his room as 'a small, warm and comfy place.' Situma served her tea. They talked with ease on various social and economic topics for about two hours. They seemed not strangers anymore; they opened up to each other easily. They shared their past experiences in life, but Situma was careful not to talk of having been jailed. At the end, he passively mentioned his visit to Muranda but did not tell her that he had gone for financial assistance.

'I visited Muranda yesterday. Unfortunately someone told him I'm in love with you. The guy roared at me to keep off you!'

'Oh… gosh what's wrong with that man? He has been stalking me for so long. That snob wanted me but I turned down his overtures long time ago. In fact, he is not trustworthy and I can't allow him to make advances towards me,' she said.

'It's true, you must be careful to fall in love with an honest partner. It will manifest the real meaning of love and make it look more of a blessing and not a punishment. Infidelity alters the significance of love and turns it into a kind of chastisement. I believe I'm trustworthy and the lady who falls for me won't regret,' he said and looked at Natasha in the eyes to see if she had understood what he meant.

'Situma, stop blowing your own trumpet!' she said and slapped him on the back. Situma held her hand and declared, 'I love you, Natasha.'

*   *   *

Their romantic affair grew by the day. Wherever Natasha was, she only thought of Situma and he too thought of her in whatever he did. He met her occasionally and they realised they were compatible in many ways, the socio-economic gap notwithstanding. Natasha had made some substantial savings which she eventually topped with a bank loan and established a hardware outlet that would be run by Situma. He quit the magazine vendor job, moved from the single room he was staying in and joined his rich lover in a high-class apartment, just like the Marai one. They began living together as husband and wife, though not legally joined.

Gossipers, amongst them Muranda, talked of Situma as a man who had been 'taken off by a woman.' He still could not believe that Situma had won Natasha's heart and they had seriously moved in together.

'Now who is the head of the house? Is it the man or the lady?' wondered Muranda.' In case they divorce, it's the man to go back to his parents but not the woman, what a circus!'

Words break no bones and the croaking of a frog does not deter a cow from drinking water, so they say. The relationship between Situma and Natasha maintained a positive trend as they gallantly showed up in public places together. After staying together for about two months, the couple planned to pay a visit to the bride's parents and later to the bridegroom's for an introduction as well as seeking marriage blessings from both families.

After a series of ups and downs, Situma was finally settling down with Natasha as his wife. Although she uplifted him from the status of a pauper to an affluent businessman, she still treated him with due respect as her husband. She was a polite woman that Situma, no doubt, was going to enjoy his stay with.

On the day of their visit to Natasha's parents, Situma was happy to travel to Karoko for the first time in a couple of years to meet his prospective in-laws. Normally an in-law is the most respected of all relatives in Situma's community. So he knew a wonderful reception awaited him at Natasha's home. I'll just be a small king in a big kingdom; he looked forward to his moment of glory.

They left Manga town very early, travelling in Natasha's sleek BMW with Situma behind the wheel. She called her mum and reported 'we are on the way.' At 11.00 a.m., they were outside the gate of a posh compound in the city waiting to be ushered in.

As they got into the home, Situma was surprised to see Musebe, his former boss at Kentem Limited, being introduced as Natasha's father. His real names were Peter Buluma, the biological father of her fiancée, Natasha Buluma. Musebe was just but an additional name, Situma later learnt. He had never imagined that Buluma was actually Musebe, who Natasha proudly talked of as a manager with an international financial organisation in the city. Situma now recalled why his former boss' documents read mostly Peter B. Musebe.

'Dad, meet my fiancée Situma Wanami, he's the one I have been talking about. He hails from Kinambi County and we're looking forward to our marriage soon,' Natasha introduced him but her father seemed not to be listening. He looked agitated and could not even shake Situma's hand.

'I don't want to hear that nonsense... you girl, looking forward to getting married to him! First, where did you get this man? No way! he banged the table and stood up, 'Natasha, is this the only suitable man you've come across in your life? Where did you meet this criminal? This choice is not a good choice. You better let go everything before it is too late,' he spat out angrily and turned sharply to Situma, 'You rogue, you criminal, keep off my daughter!'

Everybody was stunned. An expected moment of happiness turned into a sad encounter as a visibly enraged Musebe shouted at his daughter, 'You are not my daughter if you get married to this man. I will reject you!' he swore as invited friends and relatives stared at him in disbelief. His comment annoyed the mother.

'Leave the children alone provided they love each other, there's no much we can...'

'Shut up woman! This rogue cannot be entrusted to stay with our daughter! It's too dangerous to let him have her!'

Natasha's mother tried to intervene for the couple but was dramatically cut short. She got embarrassed and left the sitting room cursing. She detested the archaic idea of parents choosing partners for their children. But perhaps things would have been different if she knew the real reason behind her husband's rejection of Situma. Natasha broke down and wept. Efforts by friends and relatives to calm the situation were fruitless as Musebe stood his ground maintaining that the marriage would only go on over his dead body. The visit ended unceremoniously as Situma and Natasha took back to Manga a huge load of embarrassment mixed with rejection, instead of the much expected parental blessings.

At Manga, Natasha kept brooding over the incident at their home which she termed as a 'great letdown' by her father. She hated him for ashaming her before family members and friends who had come to greet the Mr Right. She strongly detested her father's use of what she considered foul language especially when he referred to Situma as a 'criminal.' Perhaps things would have been different if Musebe explained the reasons for his sentiments.

Situma on his part did not regret the incident. He expected such encounter especially after his turbulent and frosty relationship with Musebe during his days at Kentem Limited. He chose to explain to Natasha how he came to know her father, how they worked together, how he fired him on allegations of incompetence. Still, Situma did not reveal to

Natasha that he was once caught up in a love triangle with Musebe. And for the first time, he suggested to Natasha that they part ways following her father's strong opposition.

'It will be good for all of us – you, your dad and I – if we call off this relationship. I find it impossible to sustain... your father declared that this marriage can only take place over his dead body!' said Situma. But Natasha dissuaded him from such 'defeatist mentality' and urged him to carry on with their love regardless of the obstacles or discouragements that came their way.

'I love you Situma, whether dad likes it or not... I won't leave you. We'll stay together... I'm an adult and I can't agree to be tied down by unnecessary instructions and sloppy demands and threats from the old man. He should leave me to lead my life the way I want it with whoever I want. By the way, I discussed the issue with Mum and she told me to do what I think is right for me, not what Dad wants. She even promised to visit us soon. Be with me darling, I need you... don't go...This is just like a storm in a tea cup. It'll be over soon,' she implored Situma.

A week elapsed. They had resolved to be rebellious, defy Musebe and get married. Other family members supported them; only Musebe rejected their union. They decided to go ahead without his approval.

'The Karoko trip failed miserably. So let's try the Namufweli one. Let's go and meet my parents and inform them of our wedding plans. I'm sure they'll be supportive. Sweetie, they'll not be up in arms against my choice,' Situma assured her.

It was a Thursday. 'We shall leave here on Saturday to go and meet the old folks down in Namufweli. My mother will see and like you,' he said and pecked Natasha's cheek. 'She will welcome you and joyously dance with you. She's like a mirror; she openly shows her emotions. When she is excited everybody knows and vice versa.'

'I like such people. They are good. I hate pretenders who smile broadly when actually they are burning within.'

'But Dad is cool guy... a Minister of God... he rarely shows emotions. You need to get closer to him to discover his true feelings.'

The following day, Friday, at 10.30 a.m., Situma called the headmaster of Namufweli Primary School, the only man who owned a mobile phone in their village, and asked to speak to Mwalimu Waliaula.

'Hallo, *wandase*, this is Situma.'

'Situma, we have all along been wondering what happened to you... We were worried ... actually everybody was worried... Where are you calling from?'

'I'm in Manga, how is home?'

'We are doing fine; the old folks are fine too. Mother had malaria recently but we took her to hospital and she's now recovering. Perhaps the good news is that Catherine passed her 'A' level exams with distinctions. She has been invited to Karoko University to pursue a Bachelors Degree in Law. She scored 17 out of 19 points.'

'Congratulate her on my behalf. I'll bring her a wonderful present when I come home. By the way, Waliaula, *rekeresia*, I called to inform you that tomorrow I'll bring my fiancée home. I want her to meet the old folks and get to know all our family members before we get married.'

'You said tomorrow?'

'Yes, Saturday 10th March to be precise. Please, play the role of John the Baptist. Set the place ready for a special guest. She is a wonderful lady, the daughter of my former boss at Kentem. He does not approve of our plans but we intend to wed next month with or without his consent...'

'Hey don't steal someone's daughter,' Waliaula joked casually.

'I'm not stealing her, the mother is aware and the girl loves me head over heels.'

'Somebody once told us that he saw you selling newspapers in the streets, is it true?'

'Yes, I used to sell newspapers here, that's how I started but currently, I'm engaged in private business. We pooled some money together with Natasha, that's your *mulamwa's* name, and set up a hardware outlet in Manga town. It is good business. I will tell you more about it when I come. I even bought a vehicle, a BMW, we shall come with it tomorrow.'

'Oh, the village folks will stare at you to death.'

'Anyway, greet them all and hope to see you and talk more when we get there.'

'One more thing, Situma, Nekoye still loves you? She always asks about you.'

'Oh, poor girl. I can't be in two places at the same time. I'm technically a married man as we speak, let her get some rural folk out there and hook up. In fact, invite her to attend tomorrow's occasion so that she changes her mind and takes another step quickly. Otherwise bye for now and prepare to receive the princess of Karoko.'

*　　　*　　　*

Situma spent time in the house reading a magazine article titled 'I still love you, Mwandabi?' In the story, Mwandabi stepped out of the exam room and raised his hands in symbolic victory. He had just completed his final paper that essentially marked the completion of his Bachelor of Arts Degree in English and Literature at Karoko University.

He repeatedly shook hands with colleagues, hugged intimately and admitted that he would miss them a lot while out there. All in all, he was happy the end of college life had finally come. He always longed for the day he would leave the famous hill that stood majestically facing St. Matthew's Hospital.

Mwandabi reached his room, threw away the clipboard – a student's trademark – and dropped himself on the bed. He needed a rest after battling for three hours with a very hard poetry paper. In a relaxed mood, he thought about his girlfriend Maria and how they came to fall in love.

It was during the August holidays when he was in form six at Bamali High School and she was in form five at Manafwa School. It had rained heavily that evening in Kinambi town and some of the muddy roads were risky to walk on. Vehicles moved slowly to avoid sliding or splashing water on the humble pedestrians.

He had visited the public library to read an anthology on the works of William Shakespeare. Othello was one of the 'A' Level Literature set books. As he walked back to their house in the posh Senior Quarters, a *bodaboda* cyclist carrying a female passenger cruised past him and negotiated the sharp corner ahead at high speed. In an instant, the bicycle slid and the rider and his female passenger were tossed into the air before falling with a heavy thud in a roadside trench.

Mwandabi rushed to the scene of accident and found the lady writhing in pain as blood oozed from her injured face. The cyclist was also in deep pain as he lay prostrate in the ditch. The bicycle was extensively damaged with its round rim completely mangled. Although some angry members of the public wanted to beat the *bodaboda* man for reckless riding, Mwandabi did not concur with them as two wrongs could not make a right.

He flagged down a private car and helped rush the two accident victims to hospital. However, the Good Samaritan only dropped the patients at Kinambi District Hospital's entry and went his way. Perhaps he did not wish to involve himself in legal or financial responsibilities that could arise thereafter. The much he offered was nonetheless appreciated. With the assistance of hospital sentries, a stretcher was brought and the two patients were quickly wheeled into the wards.

Maria, the victim, was discharged three days later. Mwandabi was there to see her wobble out of the ward – an encouraging sight so far – as compared to the way she was carried in, unconscious.

A week later he again paid a courtesy call to Maria and found her basking outside their house. She was still in a convalesce state. He had brought her a soft drink and a beautiful 'Get Well' card. Just like any other schoolgirl, she appreciated and received the presents with joy. They revisited the fateful day and she thanked him a million times for saving her life. She informed him that she was a form five student at Manafwa Girls in Karoko studying Biology, Chemistry and Mathematics. He also told her about his school Bamali Boys – where he studied Literature, History and Religion.

When it was time to leave, Maria saw him off. The two walked side by side on a tiny path that led to the main highway with their bodies occasionally rubbing against each other.

'Mwandabi, you've been such a wonderful person to me. I don't know what I can offer to thank you for your kindness. I can buy you anything, I won't mind the price,' she said.

Mwandabi held her hand and spoke softly, 'I don't want anything material from you, Maria. Ever since I saw you, the unfortunate state notwithstanding, something within my heart told me that you were the woman I had been looking for. I just want your love… your whole heart,' he said. She looked at him and smiled shyly. She did not reject him outright and did not show clear signs of accepting the proposal either.

'Do you love me?' he persisted, imploring her to say something.

'I don't hate you of course, but, please, I beg we suspend this matter to another time. It's a complex one and I need some time to give you a suitable answer.'

'But I implore you to look at it positively…'

'Don't expect roses though, the answer can be either way,' she said as they parted and wished each other a good day.

The following evening as they were seated at the dining table the phone rang. His elder sister picked the receiver.

'It's your call, Mwandabi,' she said. He quickly sauntered to the phone.

'Hallo… Mwandabi speaking.'

'Hi… this is Maria, how are you doing?' the voice was soft and soothing.

'Quite fine, how is your health?'

'I'm okay, my condition has improved tremendously. In fact I called to inform you that I will be going to town tomorrow at 10 a.m. for my final medical check-ups. Will you please meet me at the hospital?'

'Sure, I will be there…'

'Bye… have a good night,' she said and ended the call.

Mwandabi remained holding the handset for a while; perhaps wishing the conversation would have continued. That night he lay on his bed wondering whether she had accepted his proposal or not. Although actions speak louder than words, he did not wish to assume things.

He met her at the hospital the next morning as agreed and he was pleasantly surprised when she rushed to meet him, with her face all smiles and hugged him. She went in to see the doctor and came out after thirty minutes. The two then strolled around the town doing some window-shopping and ended up at the Senior quarters where he introduced her to his parents as a friend. She was a presentable girl and his mother appreciated her looks and manners. Their love later picked momentum and grew stronger day by day. They wrote each other love letters while in school and promised never to part, whatsoever.

At the end of the year Mwandabi passed his final exams and secured a place at the prestigious Karoko University. After completing her 'A' level, Maria joined St. Matthew's Medical College, located next to Karoko University, for a Diploma in Nursing.

During the weekends, she spent most of her time in Mwandabi's room at the university where they talked, laughed, played and exchanged views on various aspects of life. The more they got to know each other, the more they got assured that their love was destined to succeed. After familiarisation, he proved that she was trustworthy and he vowed to dedicate all his love to her.

One memorable evening after a weekend outing to the beach, they came back late and went to Mwandabi's room. He brought a bottle of wine, poured a drink for her and himself and they toasted to the continuity of their love. Mwandabi promised never to leave her and Maria vowed to stand by him through thick and thin. Slowly but surely, they started getting tipsy and occasionally they stood up and chased each other across the room, savouring their youthful pleasures, all in the name of love.

Mwandabi remembered all these episodes with lots of nostalgia and he longed to see and talk to his sweetheart again. He had spent over three months without seeing or hearing from her. Thus, as the Kinambi bound bus cruised through the country's rough roads, he passionately thought of the wonderful reception that awaited him from his girlfriend.

They reached Kinambi town at 2.30 p.m. He immediately checked at Masaba Hospital to meet his darling. Unfortunately, he was informed, she was off duty until the following day at noon. Her colleagues, nonetheless, directed him where she stayed in the hospital quarters: Block F House number 12. He checked there, his heart throbbing with anxiety anticipating to meet his love, but she was not in. He proceeded home, dejected.

At home he was surprised to bump into a celebration where he was the chief guest. His parents had organised a welcoming party to congratulate him upon successful completion of his degree course. A couple of friends had been invited for the fete. The party ended at 8.30 p.m. to the relief of Mwandabi who got a chance to attend to personal matters. Despite the wonderful home-coming party, lavish food, drinks and presents, Mwandabi was not a happy man. He just wanted to meet Maria first. She held the key to his happiness. He mounted his Yamaha motorbike and rode to her house again. She was not back yet. He sat at her doorstep patiently for about thirty minutes but she was nowhere in sight. It was past 10.30 p.m., the town centre was deserted save for a handful of sex workers who could be spotted here and there when he returned home frustrated.

He visited the hospital again the following afternoon. 'Is Maria around?' he inquired at the reception. The answer was positive. Yes, she was there. He was told to wait as they send for her.

When she finally emerged from one of the corridors, perhaps to grace the big hour that Mwandabi had longed for, she simply gave him a cold handshake and quickly excused herself, 'Please, see me later… I'm busy with patients inside.' She proposed that they meet at 6.00 p.m. when she would be leaving work. 'Nice time,' she said passively and disappeared into the corridors, only to go back and continue chatting with her colleagues. When Mwandabi came back to the hospital at the agreed time, he found that she had already left. He quickly sensed that something was amiss. Not losing hope, he followed her to the house but she was not there either. The door was locked.

'Could I be looking for her in the wrong place?' he pondered.

'Who stays in this house?' he asked the neighbours who confirmed that it belonged to Maria but she was ever on and off.

On his way back, he met his friend Paul and told him how he had gone through hell trying to meet his love.

'Could she be dodging you?' Paul posed.

'I think she is just busy, nursing is hectic you know,' Mwandabi tried to defend her though he inwardly concurred with his friend that Maria was actually avoiding him.

'Are you sure she stays in the hospital quarters?'

'That's what I was told.'

'Did she tell you she puts up there?'

'Man, I have not talked to her yet. We did not even sit down to catch up with details… but neighbours confirmed it is her house.'

'I guess that lady puts up somewhere in Republic Estate. I have met her there severally. I cannot precisely tell the house number but I know the plot.'

'Maybe she only goes there to see a friend,' Mwandabi said contemplatively and added, 'but we can visit the place and find out more. Tomorrow is a Saturday; we may find her in the house.'

The following day at 10.00 a.m., they parked their motorbike at a gate in Republic Estate and enquired from the gatekeeper. 'Check on the first floor door number 8,' they were told. Paul led the way upstairs. They knocked slightly on the door and a female voice responded 'come in.' It was Maria's voice.

They pushed the door open and their eyes met Maria, yes, real Maria, Mwandabi's Maria. She was still in her nightdress, perhaps she had just woken up. A gentleman of about forty years, clad in a short and tight vest exposing his gigantic biceps, was seated with her at a breakfast table in an expensively furnished sitting room. The delicacies on the table were enough sign to tell that this was a house of a wealthy person, a house of means.

'Welcome guys,' she said though she was shocked to see Mwandabi. 'Have a seat,' she exercised some courtesy and inquired further, 'How did you know that I stay here?'

'We were directed from the hospital,' Mwandabi lied.

'Anyway meet my husband. He is called Namunyu, a businessman in this town,' she said and looked at Namunyu. 'Darling these guys are my friends, we studied together.'

Mwandabi was utterly surprised at the grim revelation that his love with Maria had collapsed without notice. He did not believe that she had forsaken him at an hour when he needed her most; and that she could boldly introduce him as 'a friend we went to school with.' He stood from his chair and begged to leave.

'I wish you had told me that you were married instead of giving me bouncing appointments. I could not have followed you this far, after all. Mr. Namunyu, err… Sir… sorry… I didn't mean to be a rabble-rouser in your relationship but this girl was once my girlfriend and until this morning, I knew we were still in love… this chic is cheeky!' a visibly annoyed Mwandabi said and opened the exit door with Paul trailing immediately behind him. They left the place unceremoniously.

When the two were gone, silence prevailed, and then Namunyu spoke sternly, 'Maria, I have a feeling that you are playing some nasty games behind my back. You met that ex-boyfriend of yours yesterday and you didn't tell him that things had changed? You just smiled and fixed dates? I don't want to see boys coming to my house to stage nasty scenes, be warned!' he banged the table.

'No, please, darling I cannot cheat on you. I love you and we shall be together always. I just wanted him to read my actions and see for himself that things have changed. After all, actions speak louder than words,' she said but Namunyu shook his head with misgivings. Without much ado the subject was dropped and surprisingly, Namunyu introduced the discussion of their impending one-week honeymoon retreat to the coastal city.

Later in the day, Namunyu visited the Spy Network and Private Investigations Bureau in Kinambi town and contracted them to keep a close eye on his wife's movements. He paid dearly for the service and the spy team promised to keep him updated on all her movements in and out of town: the time she enters and leaves the hospital, the salon she goes to, the café and shops she visits, the people she talks to, among other things.

Two days later, Maria went to her house in the hospital quarters, the house that she formerly stayed in before moving in with Namunyu but had not relinquished it to the hospital authorities yet. Here, she was informed of a male visitor who had frequented the place looking for her. The description they gave befitted Mwandabi. She got annoyed and decided to look for Mwandabi and warn him to keep off her. She took a *bodaboda* and headed to the Senior Quarters. She knocked on a green gate and asked the gatekeeper to call Mwandabi out.

'Please, please, please…' she raged at him when he came out, 'Keep off my life! I'm somebody's wife! How dare you look for me all over Republic Estate to come and embarrass me before my husband? You were just a good friend of mine but that did not mean that I was under any obligation to marry you. I have a right to make a choice, the choice I love. Just get yourself another girl, marry her and forget about me totally,' she spat out angrily.

'Come on Maria,' a less emotional Mwandabi moved closer and held his hand across her shoulder, 'we have been long time lovers, remember your days in St. Matthew's, we were great lovers. You promised me very many things. You promised never to leave me, you promised to marry me but you've now betrayed our love. You've pissed me down the gutter and it's now Namunyu calling the shots. Anyway, you are entitled to your choice but I have a feeling that although he is damn rich, be careful…'

'Say whatever you wish to say about him but I love him and I cannot prefer you to him. He has all that it takes; the qualities and quantities that a woman looks for in a man. The other morning you made me regret why I ever started talking to you. I never knew you were such an empty-headed man. You didn't sound like a Literature graduate from Karoko University who claims to have read hundreds of books. Grow up please and face the reality that I'm not a lady of your class. Stop trying to mix oil with water,' she sneered and walked away.

That evening, Namunyu came back with a videotape in his hand. 'Welcome darling, I guess that is another cranking movie…' she rushed to hug and peck him on the cheek as it was a routine, but he declined.

'Wait, wait, wait…' he said, biting his lips, 'watch this,' he inserted the tape into the video deck. The Spy Network unit had recorded it.

The shooting began when Maria was on a *bodaboda* in town, next came when she was knocking on a green gate and the climax of all when she was speaking to Mwandabi, with the latter's hand across her shoulder. It did not have sound elements to enable one understand what exactly transpired between the two for it had been recorded from a distance, in an undercover journalism style.

'I warned you against this boy but you still see him!'

'No, no…darling, I went to warn him to keep off me and look for…' she fumbled with words but an enraged Namunyu gave her an instant blinding slap on the face.

'You slut! damned whore! prostitute! Leave my house quickly before I do something devastating…' he roared, inched closer and made as if to give her more beating. She hastily scampered for the exit. He called her to come back and gather her belongings and cautioned her not to take anything that she did not come with; not to carry anything that he had bought for her. She owned about a dozen pairs of shoes and a wardrobe full of fashionable clothing but went away with only a pair of shoes and a handful of skirts in a small bag. She sobbed all the way to her house in the hospital quarters.

The following morning, she went back to Namunyu's house to beg for forgiveness only to find him with another woman. With a trailer-load of frustrations Maria decided to go and look for Mwandabi. She knocked on the green gate again and asked the gate keeper to call him out.

'Have you come to insult me again?' Mwandabi asked and banged the gate. She stood there and started sobbing. Paul appeared in a moment and found her crying.

'What's up Maria?'

'Why are you crying?'

'Please do me a favour, tell your friend that I want to tell him something serious. I don't intend to harm his ego either... I'm sorry for all that happened.'

'Are you sure you are sorry?' Paul asked her a little bit sarcastically as he went inside the compound to implore Mwandabi to listen to her.

'Just give her audience and hear what she has to say first. You don't need to agree with her. Just listen to what she has to tell you. She promised not to insult you and she claims it's a different matter altogether,' Paul brokered the talks.

Mwandabi finally came to her attention and amid sobs, Maria uttered the words, 'I still love you, Mwandabi.'

Situma finished reading this story and threw away the magazine. He laughed at Maria's folly but pitied Mwandabi as well.

It was 5.00 p.m. Natasha had spent the whole day in the salon making her hair. She really wanted to look smart before her prospective in-laws. Tomorrow will be the big day in Namufweli where she will officially be introduced to Situma's family.

When she came back to the house, she asked, 'darling how do I look?'

'You look wonderful.'

'Oh yes...wonderful,' she remembered the once-upon a time humorous remark that she shared with Situma when none of them imagined that one day they would sit together to discuss marriage.

'I called my brother today and told him to set the place right for tomorrow's special guest. He told me that people at home are ready to meet you. Mother will be very happy to see that I'm finally getting married. She has always been urging me on and on…'

'And what happened?'

'The right one had not come…' he pulled her close and pecked her on the cheek.

The doorbell jingled. It rang for the second and third time. Natasha stood up and headed for the door. Two smartly dressed guys – claiming to be Situma's friends – told her that they wanted to see him. Natasha went back to the bedroom to inform Situma that he had visitors but she was scared stiff when they followed her inside the bedroom while brandishing pistols.

'You are the bastard we are looking for,' one of them said pointing a gun at Situma.

'Looking for me with a gun! Oh… Please don't shoot me! Don't kill me! Take all you want…' he tried to plead with them, his hands raised in total surrender, but events happened in a twinkle on an eye. 'Don't kill me…' his cry drowned as bullets ripped through his chest. He rolled in a pool of blood. Dead.

Natasha screamed and rushed to the balcony to alert the security men but she received a heavy slap on the face as the killers tried to silence her. This was a fatal slap. The force behind the slap finished it all. It sent her toppling over the balcony and alas! She fell down, three storeys down with a thud.

The neighbours who had come out when they heard the gunshot witnessed this last scene. They could not save her life. They could not even capture those who had done all this mess. She died on arrival at Manga Hospital.

Musebe was very restless in his office regretting why he had done all that. The following day it appeared on the front pages of the daily newspapers that one of the killers had been arrested. The breaking news further revealed that Musebe had hired the thugs to kill Situma as a way of taking him away from his daughter. Musebe had paid them dearly for the job. Thus, Musebe was also arrested pending murder charges. Criminal charges for the murder of his own daughter and would–have–been son-in-law.

The news about Situma's death reached Namufweli village at the time when they were waiting for his arrival with the bride. The villagers and family members wondered whether to mourn or not for they had mourned and buried Situma at one time. This time the body was there, yes, Situma's body, but will they conduct the second burial?

Lift up your eyes in the sky
The clouds are dark and converged
Behold, the wind is blowing
And the rain is falling too...

Oh! You can feel it
Then pick up your umbrella
For there'll never be sunshine again

The sky shades tears
On its feet; the earth
The sun goes into hiding
Darkness silently approaches
The moon also picks up courage
And takes a trip over the sky;

At night
An ambitious man plans a move
But things don't go as planned
All in the strange powers of fate

Printed in the United States
By Bookmasters